Her Outback Haven

Annie Seaton

ANNIE SEATON

Her Outback Haven

Copyright © May 2019, Annie Seaton.

NOTE: This book is a work of fiction. The names, characters, places, and incidents are products of the writer's imagination or have been used fictitiously and are not to be construed as real. Any resemblance to persons, living or dead, actual events, locale or organisations is entirely coincidental.

Cover creation: Annie Seaton.

Cover photography: Jessica Burrows

Title concept: Patricia Franks

ISBN 9780648399094

HER OUTBACK HAVEN

.

Dedication

This book is dedicated to the Finlays—David and Maria, Rex and Denise— fishing buddies we met at Karumba, and now lifelong friends.

Chapter 1

'I won't be long, little mate.' Dane McDougall pushed the bowl to the back of the ute tray and tickled under the pup's chin. 'A takeaway hamburger for me and we'll have an early night ready to hit the road tomorrow.' He slammed the door of his Land Cruiser ute that he'd parked outside the pub. Dane was late, and he knew that his brothers would be impatient because they hated eating after dark. After a hard day on the boats and in the fish co-op, they were always ready to eat early. He reached into the esky, popped the top off a water bottle and filled the pup's water bowl. Bits was tied securely onto the back of his ute, with plenty of rope to move around.

It would suit him just fine to make his announcement and get out because he knew that he was going to cop some flak from his family.

Jake—his sister Jenni's partner—had guaranteed the loan, and he was the only one who knew what Dane had done, and he'd promised not to tell Jenni. Once Jenni knew any family news, she thought it needed to be shared with the other siblings, but until the deal had been finalised, Dane wanted it kept quiet.

It had been signed, sealed and delivered in the solicitor's office in Normanton this afternoon. The best part was that Mum, and her partner Rick, were home from their caravan travels for a while and had taken over the management here at the pub in Second Chance Bay. Dane knew he'd always been Mum's golden-haired boy—he'd helped out with his brothers and sister when Mum had done it tough, and she would back him against his siblings. Unfair advantage at times, but hey, his mother was savvy.

With a final pat on Bits' head, he strode through the pub, and outside to the family's usual table at the back of the grassed area overlooking the water. It was about ten minutes before sunset, and the tables were almost empty as most of the patrons—always the grey nomies and the occasional younger backpacker—jostled for the best spots over at the edge of the grass to catch a photo of the sun setting over the Gulf of Carpentaria.

Dane stood there and looked to the west. The early evening sky was magnificent, and it looked like Mother Nature was going to celebrate with him. Shards of gold, overlaid with deep violet lit the sky, and the sea held a silvery hue near the shore deepening to burnt orange as the huge golden orb headed slowly for the horizon. He couldn't keep the smile from his face as he walked over to join his family. Excitement zinged through him and he felt lighter than he had for a long time; it was hard to keep the grin off his face. He slowed his pace and shoved his hands in his pockets and reduced his walk to a casual stroll as he crossed the lawn to the table.

Jake was sitting behind Jenni and had his hands looped loosely over her pregnant tummy. Jenn had her head back on Jake's shoulder as they watched the sunset, at the same time keeping an eye on two-year-old Leni as the small girl played in the children's playground only a few metres from the table. They needn't have worried as Mum was over there on Nanny duty.

Don, the brother closest in age to Dane, and his partner, Claire, were sitting talking quietly at the end of the table. As Dane approached, Don reached up and pulled Claire closer and brushed his lips over hers.

Dane shook his head.

What the hell was happening to his family? You'd think Cupid had visited.

Not for me, he thought.

He'd had a brief relationship last year with Nicky, a girl he'd gone to high school with but all she'd wanted was the wedding ring and the noose around his neck. *And* for him to support her with all her family problems; he'd helped out as best he could and then moved on. Nicky and the whole family had left town last Christmas and moved down to Richmond and they'd lost touch.

Matt, the oldest of the four siblings at thirty-five, walked out of the bar with a tray of drinks, followed closely by Rick. 'I knew you'd be here soon, so there's a beer here for you too, bro,' Matt said.

'Thanks, I'll return the shout next time, because I'm not staying long tonight.' Dane followed them and sat on the long bench seat at the end of the table.

'Why not? It's Friday.' Matt nudged him as he put the tray on the table. 'Hot date?'

'Nope, just a little pup who wants to go home to his bed. I have an early start tomorrow.'

'Early start?' Matt frowned. 'We've got no charters on, have we?'

'No, but I've got a road trip.'

'I didn't know that.' Matt sounded peeved.

Dane reached for his beer and his voice was as dry as his throat. 'Last time I checked I wasn't aware I had to report in.'

'Jeez. Don't get your knickers in a twist. I just thought there must have been a charter I'd forgotten.'

'Nope, no charter until next Saturday. I've got a bit of a drive ahead of me tomorrow.'

'I thought you went to Normanton today?' Matt stared at him and grinned. 'My God, Dane McDougall is leaving the Bay twice in one week. You having a mid-life crisis or something? I know, there's a woman involved.'

'Don't be a smart arse.' Dane knew Matt was trying to get a rise out of him.

Don slid along the bench and joined in the conversation. 'Who's having a mid-life crisis?'

Dane rolled his eyes. 'No one.'

'Where're you off to then?' Matt looked at him curiously, and Dane understood why. It was rare for him to leave town by road; his journeys were usually by boat, out to the Gulf and work-related.

He sat back and sipped his beer with a satisfied smile. 'To my new property.' He caught Jake's eye and smiled.

'What new property?' Matt and Don spoke together, and Jenni turned around and her question followed immediately.

'Dane McDougal, you've always been the quiet one. What new property?'

9

'I'll tell you all about it when Mum comes back to the table. Then I can answer all your questions in one hit.'

Matt reached up and scratched his head. 'And what pup are you talking about?'

'My new boy. He's called Bits.'

##

Dane realised that he wasn't going to get away early like he'd wanted. By the time Mum brought Leni back to the table, and greeted everyone, the rest of the family took their time ordering their meals and they didn't beat the tourist rush to the bistro after the sunset.

Jake called to him from across the table. 'You should know this family well enough by now, mate. You're not going to get away with a hamburger and an early night. It's Friday night.'

'True.' Dane shrugged and turned to Matt. 'Order me a T-bone and chips while I go and get Bits. I can tie him up at the edge of the grass and keep an eye on him.'

Fifteen minutes later, the pup was asleep on Dane's boots under the table, the meals had been ordered, everyone had a drink, and Leni was sitting on Mum's lap at the end of the table.

Matt turned to Dane. 'Now we want to hear what you've done and all the details.'

Dane smiled. He loved winding Matt up; he was so serious. It must be the accountant genes in him. Or the oldest brother responsibility kicking in.

'Well, when I was in Normanton today, I parked behind a ute, and there was a cage in the back full of all these cute little dogs. They all looked lonely and I couldn't resist. Bits and I were made for each other.' The smile threatened to turn into a full-blown grin; he could almost hear Matt's teeth grinding.

'No, boofhead, not the dog. The new property you've bought. Is it in Normanton?'

'Nope.' Dane picked up his beer and sipped, enjoying the chorus of groans from his siblings.

'Come on, Dane,' Jenni said with a teasing smile 'Spill! This is exciting. Getting ready to look for a bride and settle down on a quarter-acre block, are you?'

Dane spluttered into his beer. 'No way. Just because you lot are all lovey-dovey lately, doesn't mean I have to do the same.'

'Dane, stop being such a torment,' his mother said but her smile was affectionate. 'Tell us what you've done.'

'I'm starting up another business.' He looked over at Matt and Donny. 'And before you get worried, I'm not going anywhere. I can link into our charters, and I think it should supplement it well.'

'So, what else do you know about besides fishing?' Matt stared at him again, and this time his frown was pronounced.

Dane sat back and folded his arms. 'Jeez, I'm overwhelmed by all of this confidence in me.'

'Be nice, son. We all just want the best for you.' His mother's voice held a little bit of censure.

Dane turned to her as surprise filled him. 'I thought you'd at least be on my side, Mum.'

'There's no sides,' she said. 'We all want to support you in . . . in whatever it is you've done. I trust all my children to make good decisions.'

Jake leaned forward. 'There's no need for anyone to worry. Dane's seen a great business opportunity, and I've backed him.'

Three stony faces looked back at him, unimpressed that Dane had shared with Jake, the brother-in-law before he'd shared with them.

'So, are you going to put them out of their misery?' Mum asked.

Dane sat back and folded his arms to match those of his siblings. 'I've bought some land a hundred kilometres up the coast.'

'Land?' The look on Matt's face was almost comical. 'How's that going to supplement the fishing?'

'I'm going to build a fishing lodge. Just south of the aboriginal land at Staaten River. A luxury, exclusive lodge.'

Matt nodded slowly. 'Not a bad idea. Could work.'

'We've talked about it for years, and I heard that Bobby Foley was selling his land, so I made an offer and he jumped at it.'

'So, have you seen the place yet?' Don asked.

'No, that's where I'm heading tomorrow. I'm going up for a couple of days. I need to look at the logistics. Things like getting the builders in, not to mention getting the frames of the buildings up there. It's a long way in, on a bad track and it's going to be expensive. And don't worry, Matt, I'll be back in time for the next charter.'

'I'm not worried about that. I'm just wondering about the wisdom of buying a place sight unseen.'

'And from Bobby Foley,' Don muttered.

Dane shot him a look.

'I didn't think there was road across to the coast around the Staaten National Park area,' Matt said.

'Not a good road, just a four-wheel drive track, but there's an airstrip. The track turns off at Dinah's Creek near the cattle station and goes south of the river to the coast. Bobby assured me it's passable with a high four-wheel drive most of the year. He was in Normanton yesterday when I signed the contract.'

'If you do go ahead with it, you could ship the building materials down from Weipa, and there are a lot of tradesmen up there too. It wouldn't be far for them to come down by boat on their days off.'

'That's what I thought,' Dane said. 'Most of the tradies in Weipa are there to make a quick buck before they head south again. They'd jump at a weekend job.'

Matt screwed his mouth up. 'So how long is the cooling-off period for the property? Will you have time to see it and get out of the contract if it's no good?'

Dane shook his head slowly. 'There were others interested, so it's been rushed through. We settled this afternoon.'

'You've settled already? Sight unseen?' Matt's voice rose almost to a squeak. 'Are you serious?'

'Oh, for God's sake, Matt. Stop carrying on, like an old woman.' Dane flicked a glance at his mother. 'Sorry, Mum, no offence meant.'

'And none taken, because I'm a long way from that.'

'Calm down, Matt. Let him tell us about it.' Don's voice was even, but Dane could see the furrow in his brow.

'It's fifty acres with deep-water frontage near the existing house. The wetland system inland is one of the last wild river systems in the world. It'll position the business for unique environmental trips too. The migratory bird life there is amazing.'

'Does anyone live close to it?' Jenni asked.

'No, there's just the rough fishing camp with limited facilities at Dinah Creek about fifteen kilometres inland, and there's a small aboriginal settlement about sixty kilometres north.'

'Sounds isolated,' Matt said, but he looked a bit less worried. 'I'm not going to ask you how much you paid for it, but—'

'Good, because it's none of your damn business.'

'But,' Matt continued as though he hadn't been interrupted. 'What sort of condition is the house in? Can you do it up or is it a knock-em-down?'

'That's what I'm going up to see. I'm thinking if it's in a fit state to live in, I could let the builders stay there instead of camping out while they build the new lodge.'

Don nodded, and Dane waited.

'Well, I think the idea's got merit. We could do a charter, and combine the Gulf fishing with barra fishing in the Staaten River. And like you said we could venture into ecological and birdwatching trips too. It's pretty much untouched.'

'Thanks, Donny,' Dane said.

'No, don't go thanking me. I've still got reservations. If Bobby Foley's involved, there'll be a scam somewhere. Are you sure it's his to sell?' Don asked.

'Yes. I know what he's like, so I asked the solicitor to double-check. Apparently, the house was an outpost of a small mission back in the early 1900s. The Anglicans had a mission up at Kowanyama, and Bobby said there's an old church there too, but it's a ruin. It's been in his family since the 1940s. He grew up out there and they worked on the cattle station.'

'Well, I think it sounds fabulous.' Mum leaned over and squeezed his arm. 'I'm proud of you, Dane.'

Chapter 2

Nicole peeked in on Binnie; she was sound asleep in her bed on the enclosed veranda and as always, the surge of love that filled Nicole's chest as she looked at the child was physical. Plump cheeks were pink from the hour they'd spent building castles in the sandpit before lunch, and dark lashes framed eyes shut tightly as the beautiful little girl slept.

Leaving the door ajar, Nicole hurried around to the other side of the verandah. She barely spared a glance for the silvery blue sea or the deep clear sky, her thoughts were already on the order she had received last week. A light breeze blew in from the water, keeping the temperature to a reasonable level; she wasn't looking forward to the heat and humidity that was only a couple of months away. Their first summer last year in the Gulf had been a shock, but after a few months, they had both acclimatised. One thing, there was never a shortage of tank water, and she and Binnie had spent many an afternoon in the plastic blow-up pool in the

17

shade around the back of the house under the brilliant red Poinciana tree.

Binnie should sleep until four, so it would give her a chance to get started on the new commission. Nicole paused by her supplies table under the shuttered windows that faced the Gulf. A bag of untouched clay sat there, and her ever-present guilt kicked in. She should have been working nights to get the Information Centre order done. The deposit had been much needed, and the balance of the payment would see them through the next few months. It was almost time for a trip to Normanton to stock up the pantry.

The clay sat there looking at her accusingly.

'All right, all right, I'm coming.' She crossed to the table and picked up the bag of kaolin clay. It would be much easier not to have to mix her own, but moist clay weighed a lot more, and she couldn't afford the shipping these days. She was just lucky that she'd had some of her equipment in Laura's car before—

Nicole pulled a shutter down on those thoughts. She'd followed the advice of her high school art teacher, and she was happy with where she was now.

Where *they* were now.

'Life can be like a lump of clay; if you don't mould and shape it into something, it will sit like a lump on the table until someone does something with it or throws it away,' Mrs Hart had said. Her lessons had never been boring, and she had recognised Nicole's talent and had nurtured her. Both artistically, and as a life mentor, through a difficult time.

'Extend yourself. Don't be boring. Clay is never boring. There's always more to explore, and more to create. Life is like pottery; a great adventure as deep and broad as the earth that the clay comes from.'

Nicole knew she'd thrown away her life by making wrong choices. Her only regret was that she couldn't contact Mrs Hart and let her know she was okay now. It wasn't worth the risk.

But having Binnie in her life had come from that wrong choice, and she would go back and make the same decisions again for that very reason. Maybe her later decisions would have been different. Binnie's confidence had gone ahead in leaps and bounds over the past year; the isolation had healed them both.

Almost.

Nicole lifted the scales from the shelf behind her main work table. The downside of working with dry clay was the mixing, and she couldn't afford a clay mixer. It meant that she didn't need to work out to stay fit; even though she was thin, the muscles in her arms were stronger than they'd ever been in the days when she'd paid a fortune for membership at the flash gym in Melbourne.

She paused as she opened the plastic bag and tilted her head. A frown pulled at her forehead as she let go of the bag and crossed to the louvre window beside the door. Dust was hanging above the road as a vehicle approached the turnoff to the driveway to the house.

Her hand went to her pocket and her breath stilled; the car keys were still on the kitchen table at the back of the house. She usually made sure they were in her pocket.

I've become too complacent.

The old Subaru she'd changed Laura's car for in Gympie on the trip north was locked away in the shed at the side of the house. Nicole hurried quietly through to the kitchen and picked up her keys and purse, ready to grab Binnie and flee to the shed if it became necessary. It had been weeks since the last vehicle had gone past the house, and she'd been relieved when it hadn't stopped but continued south, the roof basket of the off-road vehicle filled with tents, jerry cans and fishing rods.

Tiptoeing to the front door, she glanced along the western verandah as she stood there.

Binnie was still asleep, she'd rolled over and her face was buried in the pillow.

At least the house looked deserted from the outside. The mess in the yard and under the house bugged her, but she'd always figured it was safer to leave it like it was.

Neglected and looking as though the house was unoccupied. Although with squatters around, that was a risk in itself.

She stood there and held her breath again as the rising dust came closer to the gate.

Keep going, go past, keep going, she willed the vehicle. Biting her lip, indecision filled her; stay in the house, or grab Binnie and sneak down the back stairs to the shed?

The white four-wheel drive ute slowed and turned into the gate, and her stomach clenched. She gripped her keys tightly and waited, with the occasional glance at Binnie as the ute approached the house and slowed. Her leg muscles tightened as she got ready to run, and a bead of sweat rolled slowly down her forehead.

The ute came closer and she clenched her jaw until a small measure of relief lightened Nicole's worry. She could see the logo on the side: **McDougal Fishing Charters-Second Chance Bay.**

She'd heard of them, and they were more likely to be here for a reason that had nothing to do with her. As long as she and Binnie stayed silent, and they didn't come to the house.

Nicole's breathing eased, but she stood silently behind the closed door, taking care to step back into the shadows where she couldn't be seen. With a bit of luck, whoever it was would walk down to the water and not stay too long. Mr Foley had told her it was a deep-water frontage, great for launching fishing boats when she'd signed the lease, but no one had turned up with a boat in the months since they'd arrived.

The car pulled up with a crunch of wheels on the gravel driveway at the front. She pressed herself against the wall, keeping her gaze on Binnie as a door slammed.

She slept on without a murmur and Nicole stood silently.

Waiting. Waiting for the tread of footsteps on the rickety double stairway at the front of the house.

But there was nothing. No sound. No footsteps. No voices.

She leaned forward and looked through the half-closed louvres. A tall man with broad shoulders was bending down to something at his feet, a fair way from the house, halfway between the vehicle and the water. She put her fingers on the glass slats and stared; his back was to her and he was too far away to see her even if he did turn around. She narrowed her eyes as a high-pitched yip reached her and then the man walked slowly away, holding a lead. A tiny little black ball of fur plonked its bottom in the middle of the path and the man stopped again. He was close enough for her to hear his chuckle as he tugged on the lead.

'Come on, Bits. Don't tell me you're scared of crocodiles. Fine fishing companion, you'll make.' His words drifted across through the window as he called to the dog. After a few seconds of non-cooperation on the dog's part, the man walked back, bent down and scooped the pup into his arms and walked towards the shoreline.

Nicole was relieved, but she still didn't want him to know that there was anyone living in the house.

Fishing. But why was he here? So far away from Second Chance Bay.

As far as she knew, no one knew they lived here, except for Mr Foley, their landlord; he'd promised to be discreet when she had asked him not to mention she was living here. Each time she went to town, she went to a different store and didn't get into conversation with anyone.

Tried to look like a tourist.

The highest risk was picking up her supplies at the post office, but she always had them sent with the instruction to be collected at Normanton Post Office, which ensured her anonymity.

No address on record, and she'd gone back to her mother's maiden name. The only problem was it made it difficult to sell her pieces because she'd been so well-known as Nicoletta Spagnolo—Bruno had insisted she use that name as he was sponsoring her—when she'd won the first award. It had meant starting from scratch here as Nicole Curtis, but the commissions had been coming slowly as she'd emailed various catalogues from a generic email account that gave her anonymity. And Bruno had been so self-centred, he'd never even met her mother or asked about her, so he wouldn't know the name.

She hoped.

Nicole leaned forward and waited. The man spent a long time down at the water's edge, looking along the beach, and Nicole relaxed a little as she walked to the back of the house. Binnie was still asleep, so she made her way to the kitchen, where she could get a better view of him as he walked further away from the house She frowned as she went into the large open kitchen; she'd forgotten she'd left the window open, so the breeze would flow through the house. It was too late to close it now, that would just draw his attention. She watched as he picked his way along the shoreline, getting further away from the house with each step.

Her heart was still beating fast, and a dull ache tugged at her chest.

Please hurry up and go, she begged silently. The tension kicked back in and Binnie would wake up soon. She didn't want her to be frightened; it had taken months to win her confidence after—

Tears welled in Nicole's eyes; she wouldn't go there.

***

The deep-water frontage was much better than Dane had expected. A small jetty built out into the middle of the bay would cater for boats the size of Jake's *Moonshine* and *Starshine* with no trouble at all even if the tide was low. If he took Matt's advice and shipped the building equipment in by boat, the water was deep enough to take a commercial vessel. Much of the Gulf was shallow, as many skippers found when they came aground on sand shoals in seemingly deep water.

It was only a kilometre or two from here to the mouth of the Staaten River and the river was deep and wide. Up in the Kimberleys where Don had worked charters recently—and where Don had met Claire— the accommodation was inland, and the guests had to be taken to the boats by coach.

Dane decided to go and find the airstrip here after he checked the house out.

So far it was looking great, and he was happy with what he'd paid for it, now that he'd seen that the land around the house was high, and well away from the wetlands.

Excitement filled him; the same old fishing charters they'd been doing since their father had established the business in the eighties had become routine and monotonous. Now Don had his charters up in the Kimberley, and Jake's boats had added an upmarket edge to the existing charters out of the Bay. Dane had been taking out the original family boats—the *Sally M* and the *Elsie* were both tired and in need of refurbishment—and he was ready for a change too.

This was an ideal location; he could picture the buildings set back a little way from the water. They could fly the guests into the airstrip, cater for them at the lodge and take them out on a day trip. He'd install a commercial kitchen in a separate building and hire a good chef. If he was going to do this, he'd do it well. With Jake as a silent partner and his local fishing knowledge, Dane knew he could make this an upmarket luxury adventure experience.

Next stop was the house; the main question would be—demolish or refurbish?

He turned to head back to the house; the keys to the front door were in the ute.

His neck prickled, and he stopped and looked up; a curtain was blowing at an open window. For a moment it had looked as though someone was standing there. He shrugged, put Bits down when he started to whimper and walked back to the ute, but keeping his eyes on the house.

It was an incredible building; maybe he *would* keep it. A Queenslander with a magnificent red tree in full bloom overhanging the rusted roof sat close to the beach. The grass was long around the house; broken and rusted tools were scattered around the front yard and old pieces of machinery were under the house. It looked as though no one had lived there for years. Old cane furniture sagged on the verandah that wrapped around two sides of the house. Lace curtains filled the two front windows and a small tree had pushed through the railing on the old-fashioned staircase that came down from the verandah in a line with the front door, and then split to the left and right.

He wondered what he would find inside; mostly rats and bird droppings with that window open, he guessed. It would have been a magnificent house in its day, but it would take a lot of money—and work—to restore the place to its former glory.

Dane looked up as a loud creak pierced the stillness of the early afternoon. With a frown, he stared at the house as the front door opened.

Bloody hell. There was someone inside!

Squatters. He'd soon move them on.

He stood there frowning as a small girl ran down the stairs and hurried towards him, a wide smile on her face as she headed for Bits.

'Binnie. No! Come back now!' The cry was shrill and loud.

Dane looked back to the house. A slightly built woman with fair hair was hurrying down the side of the stairs closest to where he stood with Bits.

The puppy yapped as the little girl crouched down beside them and held her hand out. She giggled when Bits' wet nose touched her hand, and when his little pink tongue licked her fingers, she giggled again.

'Hello. Are you Binnie?'

The little girl looked up at Dane with wide eyes. The woman hurried across and reached down and took the little girl's hand. She pulled her away and gently pushed her behind her.

'How do you know her name?' Her voice was soft, but her gaze was like steel as she stood protectively in front of the child.

Dane straightened his shoulders and stared back at her. She was almost as tall as he was. 'I didn't. I assumed that was her name because you called it from the steps.'

'I want you to leave our land now.'

'Your land?' Dane stared at her. It was like one of those westerns he'd loved as a kid; all the woman needed was a shotgun on her shoulder pointing at him, and the image would have been perfect.

'Yes.' She folded her arms and glanced nervously back at the house as though she was measuring the distance to get away from him. 'My husband is asleep. He . . . he went fishing all night. Drive out quietly, so you don't wake him up. Come on, Binnie.' She reached down and picked the child up and turned back to the house.

'Wait.' Dane put his hand out and the woman jumped as his fingers brushed her shoulder.

She turned slowly.

'Mrs. . .?

'Curtis,' she said.

'I'd like to speak to both you and your husband. Together.'

'Why?' Her voice was wary. When she glanced back at the house again Dane realised it was fear that filled her eyes. Her shoulders were stiff, and her jaw was tight.

He stepped back and put his hands up. 'I'm sorry, Mrs Curtis. Let me start again. My name is

Dane McDougal. We have a fishing charter business at Second Chance Bay.' He gestured to the ute. 'As you can see on my vehicle.'

'Why do you need to talk to me? To us, I mean?'

'Because I was told that no one lived here and that this house—my house—was empty.'

'Your house?' She shook her head. 'It's not your house. We live here.'

'You're squatting.'

Her voice rose as she stared at him. 'No! We're not squatters. We rent off Mr Foley. He's the owner.'

Dane nodded. 'Mr Bobby Foley *was* the owner. He was the owner before he sold me this land and this house. So, I need to speak to both you and your husband about vacating the premises as soon as possible. I'm the new owner and I have plans for the house.'

To Dane's utter consternation, her eyes filled with tears. The woman—Mrs Curtis—bowed her head and put her free hand up to her face.

'No.' Her cry was full of anguish.

Chapter 3

Nicole had no doubt that Dane McDougal of McDougal Fishing Charters was telling the truth. She also had a three-year lease signed and the receipt paid for the rental of the house until the end of next year.

Embarrassed by the tears that had sprung to her eyes, she brushed away at them with one hand. Binnie wriggled in her arms and grunted.

'Go upstairs, Binnie. Wait for me on the verandah.' She slid down Nicole's legs and walked across to the stairs.

Nicole smiled at Binnie to dispel the obvious tension. No matter what the little girl lacked, she was observant—and obedient.

Usually.

The man waited until Binnie had climbed up the steps with a wistful look back at the puppy.

'Can we go inside? Or perhaps I can wait on the verandah while you get your husband.' He ran a hand through his hair as she watched him, his frustration obvious.

'Please give me a moment while I get Binnie a drink. She's not long woken up.' Nicole shook her head. She hadn't realised that Binnie could reach the door latch. Horror flooded through her at the thought that she may have wandered outside one night. Although it was beautiful in its isolation, the property was fraught with danger. Nicole could live with the huge spiders that sometimes found their way inside, but she was always very wary of the snakes and the crocodiles that she knew were out there. For someone who'd grown up in the city, she was very proud of how she'd coped up here.

So far.

Even during the category one cyclone that had threatened last year, she'd managed to cope and kept them safe.

Safety.

That was all she needed. As time passed, the threat from Melbourne would pass.

It would.

'So?' The man's voice was quiet.

He was staring at her with a strange look on his face.

'I'm sorry, what did you say?'

'Can I wait on the verandah while you get your husband?'

Nicole bit her lip, wondering what to do.

Or say.

'Yes, please come up to the verandah.' She strode towards the house and hurried up the stairs ahead of him. Gesturing to the small cane setting near the door, she watched as he followed her up the stairs. 'Please take a seat. It's stronger than it looks.' As much as she hated to offer, good manners prevailed. 'Can I offer you a cup of tea?'

'Thank you, that's very kind,' he said.

She waited until he sat at the table and pushed open the front door and took Binnie inside. She sat her at the kitchen table and crossed to the camping fridge.

'You stay there. Mummy was worried when you opened the door.'

Binnie nodded.

Nicole reached for the juice and the carton of long-life milk. 'Juice or milk?' She held them both up. Binnie pointed to the juice and Nicole reached for a plastic mug. Once she had put the drink in front of Binnie and added a couple of biscuits to a plate on the table, she turned and filled the kettle, her mind working furiously.

Could she believe him when he said that he hadn't known she was here? How could Mr Foley have sold the house and not mentioned it was tenanted? She frowned as she waited for the water to boil. To be fair, she had asked Mr Foley not to tell anyone she was here, but she also hadn't expected that he'd sell the house.

Panic clawed at her stomach, and as Nicole reached up for the cups and teapot her hands were shaking. There was nowhere to go, and they couldn't move because there was no money. They had enough to buy groceries and pay the car registration and insurance when they came due. The rent included the electricity, and the deposit on the recent commission had been enough to order the clay.

The credit on her internet dongle had run out, and she'd not been able to check her email for two weeks; that was on the list when they went to Normanton next week. The library internet was free, so she'd decided to use that from now on.

The kettle whistled, and Nicole poured the boiling water onto the tea bags. Adding sugar and milk and another plate of biscuits to the tray, she turned to Binnie. 'When you finish your drink, you can go and play for a little while, but I want you to stay inside. Okay?' She reached down and hugged the little girl, burying her face in the sweet-smelling hair.

'Okay?' she repeated when she stood straight.

Binnie nodded.

'I'll talk to the man, and have my tea, and then I'll call you. You stay inside until I call, and then you can say goodbye to the puppy. Right?'

Again, the sweet nod. Nicole's heart clenched; she would give anything, do anything to hear that sweet little voice again.

Damn you, Bruno Spagnolo.

She crossed to the cupboard where she kept her papers and pulled out the informal letter that had served as a lease, and the handwritten receipt showing she had paid three thousand six hundred dollars for three years rent. It was probably the only place in Australia where you could rent a house for twenty-four dollars a week. She put it on the table in case he insisted on seeing it.

She might not be able to do anything about Binnie not talking for twelve months, one week and three days—the date was fixed in Nicole's head for life—but she would fight tooth and nail to keep a roof above their heads.

A roof she had paid good rent for.

***

Bits had gone to sleep in Dane's lap and his fingers smoothed the little pup's coat while he waited for the woman to come out of the house with her husband. All was quiet, and he could hear no voices. Finally, the door opened, and she emerged carrying a tray set with two cups, a pot of tea, a sugar bowl and a jug of milk.

She set it carefully on the table and pulled out the other chair, her head down. There was no sign of the little girl—or a husband. Dane glanced at his watch. He had intended to travel down to the campground at Dinah's Camp and sleep in his swag after he'd checked out the house, but if he didn't get going soon, it would be too late to travel there. He didn't know the road well enough to traverse it in the dark. He looked at the tray and then up at Mrs Curtis.

'Is your husband still sleeping?'

Her reply was quiet and surprised him. 'Do you have any identification to prove you are who you say?'

Dane stood, put Bits on the chair and pulled his wallet from his back pocket and removed his driver's licence. He passed it over to her. 'Photo ID.'

She took it from him, and he was surprised again to see her hands shaking as she looked at the photo and then up at him. She passed it back without a word. He returned it to his wallet and then to his pocket and sat down again, leaving Bits on the other chair. He hadn't stirred.

She lifted the teapot and filled a cup with a hot strong brew just as he liked it.

'Milk? Sugar?' She tipped her head to the side and it was as though they were having a normal friendly afternoon tea.

An eerie light surrounded them as the sun went behind a cloud, and the wind whistled around the corner of the house from the sea. Some loose sheets of iron banged above their heads. There was no sound or sign of life from inside.

When she had poured her tea, she pushed the plate of biscuits towards him, but he shook his head.

'Maybe the pup would like one.'

Dane smiled and reached for a biscuit and put it beside the pup. Bits' nose twitched but he stayed asleep.

'Thank you, Mrs Curtis,' Dane said. It was obvious that his presence had unsettled her, so he waited for her to start the conversation. It was a strange setup here.

She sipped her tea and he waited her out. Finally, she put the cup on the table and looked at him. Her skin was fair, like her hair and there were a couple of fine lines around her eyes. Her hair was pulled back from her high forehead in a ponytail. Her blue eyes were tired and fringed with long lashes, but it was the shadows beneath them that he noticed more.

'Please call me Nicole.' She lifted her head and his gaze brushed her long and slender neck. 'I'm not going to beat around the bush. After I tell you why we *must* stay here, I'm going to beg. If I tell you the truth I hope that you'll allow us to stay here for as long as I've paid the rent.'

Dane went to speak, but she put a shaking hand up. 'Please hear me out. There's one thing I need you to promise me. What I am going to tell you has to stay between us. No one else can know we're here.'

'I'm not sure if I can promise that at this point.' Dane held her intent gaze. He was used to the various characters who came and went in the Gulf. For those who wanted to disappear, it was a wild frontier where it was very easy to drop out of society. 'Tell me why you're here.'

'Binnie and I live here by ourselves. I have no husband. There is no one asleep inside like I said before. It's just the two of us.' Her voice was matter-of-fact, but her eyes were sad. 'We're here so I can keep Binnie safe.'

Dane couldn't help interrupting. 'There's just the two of you, way out here? On your own?'

She nodded.

'But that's *not* safe. What if you had an accident? Or you or your child got sick? It's hours from Normanton to here. Do you have a car? Or do you travel by boat?'

'I know. I have a four-wheel drive in the shed over there.'

A frisson of sympathy niggled at his chest, but Dane pushed it away. He'd got too close to Nicki's family issues—it must go with the name; her full name was Nicole too—and he'd pulled back before he'd become too involved. But her family issues there had been nothing as serious as a woman and a child living so far from anywhere. Alone.

'Okay, I understand that you seem to want to disappear, and I'll accept that. But why can't you move somewhere else?'

'In one word? Money.' She shrugged but her dark brown eyes remained on his. 'I've paid rent for this house until the end of *next* year, and I have a lease signed by Mr Foley. I can show you. I shouldn't have to leave. And the bottom line is I can't afford to leave. So I'm begging you to let us stay.'

'Yeah, Bobby Foley. I'm sorry to be the one to tell you, but he's one of the greatest con artists in the Gulf. He neglected to tell me that the house had tenants when he sold it to me.' Dane shook his head as frustration filled him; he'd always been a soft touch, but this was a situation where he was going to have to be firm. 'Look, Nicole, I'd love to help

39

you out, but the bottom line is, I have business commitments. I've taken out a substantial loan to develop a business based here, and like you, there is one word for me to consider too. *Money.* I can't afford to wait until the end of next year before I build the lodge and get my business up and running. I need to see a return on my investment.'

Her shoulders went rigid, and a wave of fear crossed her face. He was horrified when her eyes filled with tears, and she put a shaking hand up to her face. Dane was a sucker for tears, he always had been. Jenni had known how to get her own way when they were kids, but this time he knew the tears weren't put on. The woman was clearly terrified.

'Look,' he said gently. 'I know you said there was a money issue, but what if I found you somewhere to live back in Second Chance Bay? I know where there's an empty house. My brother's partner was living there for a while, and now it's empty.' The Dunstan house had been vacant since Claire had moved in with Donny.

'But it's in a town where there are people, and people are curious about where you come from. I can't afford for that to happen. She lifted her head and her face was stark with an expression that was hard for Dane to understand. 'I have to stay here.'

Her expression broke his heart.

Grief? Fear?

Chapter 4

It was strange to be sitting on the verandah and having a conversation with another adult. Nicole could count on one hand the number of conversations she'd had over the past year.

With adults anyway.

Although she made sure that she spoke to Binnie constantly, and she knew the little girl understood her, her speech had not returned. She could follow Nicole's instructions and sometimes it appeared she was going to speak, and then her little face would cloud over, and she would close her lips tightly. Her development was normal; Nicole had read all the articles on loss of speech due to trauma at the library, and she prayed that one day the words would come back. In the meantime, they took one day at a time and she was reassured by Binnie's development and her ability to understand what Nicole was saying.

She didn't need a child psychologist to tell her what had caused it.

41

The day that Binnie had stopped talking remained etched in her memory. She shivered; even thinking about it filled her with terror.

It could have been Binnie. It could have been her. Or both of them.

'Nicole?' The deep voice was gentle as it pulled her from her thoughts. 'Are you with me?'

'I'm sorry.' She took a deep breath trying to calm herself, but the events of the afternoon and the fear that had filled her when he'd driven up the drive were hard to shake. 'What did you say?'

'I said why can't you afford for people to see you?'

'I meant risk, not afford. But please don't worry, Mr McDougal, I'm not a criminal.'

'It's Dane.'

'Then don't worry, *Dane*. Like I said, I'm not a criminal.' Nicole picked up her teacup and stared at it, so she didn't have to see the expression that she imagined would be on his face.

'But you're hiding?'

'I am. We are. We have to.'

There was silence between them for a while and finally, he let out a sigh. 'Look I know you're entitled to privacy, but if—and only if, I am going to consider letting you stay for a while, I need to know more.'

'Fair enough,' she said.

'I mean, is it going to impact on my land or my business if what—or who—you're so scared of, finds you? I need to know.'

The buzzing in her ears should have warned her, but Nicole pushed herself up from the chair as her heart began to beat furiously. Her mouth dried and the last thing she was aware of, was Dane lunging for her with his arms held wide.

***

Dane pushed the door open with his shoulder, aware that the little girl was inside somewhere. He'd known Nicole was going to faint as soon as she'd stood; her face had gone chalk-white and her eyes had rolled back in their sockets. He'd been fast enough to catch her as she'd crumpled back down towards the chair. He'd scooped his arms beneath her legs and made sure her head was supported by his shoulder before he headed for the door. She was a featherweight, and as he carried her he could feel the gauntness of her frame that he hadn't noticed under the loose trousers and long shirt before she'd ended up in his arms.

A surge of sympathy stuck in his throat.

What a life.

Hiding out here, with just a small child for company; it had to be a domestic violence issue.

'Binnie,' he called softly. 'Are you there?'

The small girl came down a long dimly-lit hallway that led to the back of the house. Her eyes widened when she saw him, and she backed away, her eyes wide. She pressed herself against the wall and put her hands over her face.

'It's okay, sweetheart.' Dane kept his voice soft and even. 'Mummy was feeling a bit sick and I'm taking her to the sofa to lie down. Can you show me which room is the lounge room?'

As the little girl pointed to the door to his left, Nicole began to stir.

'Wha—' She stiffened in his arms as her eyes opened and she looked up at him.

'It's okay. You fainted. I'm just looking for a sofa to lie you down.'

'We don't have one,' she mumbled as she blinked a few times. A little bit of colour had come back into her cheeks and he could feel the steady beat of her heart against his arm. 'Just our beds.'

'Which room?' he asked, keeping an eye on Binnie as she crept cautiously towards him. He didn't want to scare her.

'The bedroom. Across the hall.' Nicole's voice was still weak, and Dane changed direction, following her instruction. He pushed open the door and as he walked in, there was a sharp tug on the back of his long-sleeved shirt at the same time a little foot kicked his leg.

'Put her down. I want my Mummy. Now.'

He looked down as Nicole pushed at him, her hands strong. 'Oh my God. Oh my God, Binnie.' Her voice shook, and tears spilled from her eyes. She pushed herself away from Dane and her feet went to the floor.

'What's the matter? Are you ill again?' He tried to hold her, but she turned away. She shook her head and dropped to a crouch, her arms going around the little girl, her chest heaving with sobs.

'Binnie, oh Binnie. Say it again.'

'Don't let the big man hurt us.' The little voice was quiet but shaking.

Regret pierced Dane's chest as he stood there, unsure of what was happening. He didn't want to move and frighten the little girl any more than she was; she was obviously terrified. He looked around the room as Nicole rocked the small girl in her arms.

Two single mattresses lay side by side on the floor near the window, and a suitcase and three boxes sat in a neat line along the wall. His eyes narrowed as he took in the spartan nature of the room. He hadn't taken any notice of the rest of the house as he'd carried her inside.

45

Nicole's little girl was still clinging to her, and he stepped back to give them privacy. The little girl's arms were tight around her neck and Nicole had her face against the small head.

'I'll wait in the kitchen,' he said quietly. Nicole lifted her head and the expression on her face wrenched at his heart. It was full of joy, but tears were rolling down her cheeks. There was something going on here that he didn't understand.

Chapter 5

Nicole's legs trembled as she walked along the hall, holding tightly to Binnie's hand. The joy of hearing that little voice for the first time in over a year lightened her step and pushed away the immediate worry of potentially losing the house. Dane McDougal was a kind man, he had shown that in his concern for them already.

Maybe they could talk, *really* talk. Maybe he would understand.

He was standing at the window looking thoughtful as he stared out at the Gulf. The light was fading quickly as it did in the tropics and she flicked the light switch on.

'How about another cuppa?' she said brightly. 'My mum always said it was the cure for all ills.'

'Thank you. That would be good. Are you feeling okay now?' He walked across to the table and two chairs and for the first time, Nicole looked at him as he pulled out the chair and sat.

Really looked.

He was a tall man with a rugged face, clean-shaven, but obviously overdue for a haircut. Mid-brown hair tipped with blond brushed his collar. Her eyes travelled down to broad shoulders; his hands were strong, and a flush of warmth travelled up her neck as she remembered being in his arms.

'Mummy?'

Nicole's smile was so wide it tugged at her cheeks. 'Yes, sweetheart.' She was still holding Binnie's hand.

'Can I have some juice, Mummy? Please.'

She let go of her little girl's hand and her fingers caressed Binnie's hair before she crossed to the small camping fridge in the corner of the large room. 'You can have whatever you want today. It's just a shame we're due for a shopping trip. We need to have a celebration tonight.'

Dane's hands were flat on the table as he leaned back in the chair. She was conscious of him watching her every move, but she felt comfortable in his presence. She had gradually gotten used to having another person inside the house with them. 'While I get our drinks, how about you show Mr McDougal your drawing.'

She smiled as Binnie walked purposefully around the table and gathered her precious colouring book. For a child her age—she would be five in February—she was already showing artistic

48

talent, passed down from Nicole. The back of each colouring page was filled with her little drawings

Nicole's breath caught as Binnie spoke clearly. 'This is a cow, and this is a boat.'

Dane lowered his head and looked at each page. Nicole turned away, biting her lip to hold back the emotion and filled the kettle again. Once she had herself under control, she said, 'I'll just go out and get the tray.' She didn't want to tell him she had only two teacups. When they had fled Melbourne, she had left with only the clothes on their backs, some of her tools, her purse and Laura's car. After three weeks of driving as far away from Melbourne as she could get, they'd ended up in Normanton. Once they had found the house to live in and had paid the rent, Nicole had been very frugal with what was left. The tea set comprising a pot, two cups and the milk jug and sugar basin had been a one-dollar find at the op shop in town, along with a few other basic necessities the day they had passed through Normanton on the way to the house.

Listening to Binnie talk to Dane as she showed him her drawings were incredible. Maybe it was having someone else in the house that had unblocked whatever it was that had been holding her silent. Maybe it had been the shock of Nicole fainting, it was hard to guess, although she knew full well the cause of Binnie's silence. Goosebumps crept up Nicole's arms. She put the cups into the sink and rinsed them, and then emptied the tea leaves into the bucket.

As she turned to the window, she was taken aback by how dark it was. 'Where has the day gone? It's teatime, young lady.' She swallowed and looked at Dane, framing the question she didn't want to ask. 'Would you like to stay for dinner? I'm afraid we're having fish. You probably get sick of that.'

He hesitated for a moment and then he smiled. 'Only if you will let me contribute. I have a fridge the same as yours'—he gestured to the camp fridge— 'in the back of the ute. 'More food in it than I'll eat in a couple of nights.'

'Where are—were—you going to stay tonight? We've really held you up here.'

'I was heading for Dinah's Camp, but if you don't mind, I'll drive up to the other end of the beach and camp out in my swag. It's a bit late to drive across the wetlands. I'd hate to go off the road into the soft ground.'

'You're most welcome to bunk out on the verandah tonight. I'm very grateful for your help today. More than you'll ever know,' she added quietly looking at the top of Binnie's head. 'Why don't you go and get whatever you want to heat up while I bath this little one, and cook her some eggs.'

'Mummy?'

Nicole fought the lump in her throat; she'd shed enough tears today to last a lifetime. 'Yes, sweetie,' she replied as Dane stood.

'We didn't get the eggs from the chicken pen today.'

'You have a chicken pen?' he asked. 'I didn't see it.'

'It's about a hundred metres through the bush. I built it up high on stilts and we have a small veggie garden there too. Just enough to keep us going between visits to Normanton. Along with the fish we catch, we're pretty self-sufficient here.'

He shook his head as he headed for the door. 'You are.'

Nicole stood staring at the door for a long time after it closed behind him.

##

Dane took his time at the ute to give Nicole time to bath Binnie. Before he'd come outside he'd checked to make sure the colour had come back into her face, with no chance of her flaking out again. She'd jumped up suddenly; maybe it was lack of food that had caused her to faint. He frowned, trying to remember what they had been talking about when the colour had left her face. He'd asked her what impact it would have on his business if whoever she was hiding from turned up.

The look of fear that had crossed her face in that instant had stayed with him. It was clear she had good reason for hiding herself out in this wild country. Dane shook his head as he pulled out the slide under the camping fridge. It wasn't safe—a woman and a small child out here, no matter what they were hiding from.

What if there was an accident? Or if one of them got sick? Snake bite? What if Nicole cut herself while she was building chook pens or something? She could bleed to death and leave a small child out here alone.

He shook his head again, unable to believe the risk she was taking. He couldn't condone someone living out here like that now that he owned the place. It would be irresponsible.

There was no medical facility within a hundred kilometres. The odds of something happening out here were high. Plus, some rogue characters made their way to the Gulf and squatted in empty houses. Nicole had been lucky that he'd turned up and not someone with fewer scruples.

No, he couldn't allow her to stay here. Whatever her problem was, it wasn't any of his business. He'd do anything he could to help them move on, but he wouldn't sleep at night knowing there was a woman and a small child out here on a property he owned.

Dane turned his attention to the plastic containers in the small fridge. One was labelled "Curried Chicken" and the other "Beef Goulash". Knowing his mother, there would be enough in each to feed an army let alone one woman. Hell, he'd pulled in fish that weighed more than she did.

He pulled out the gas bottle with the heating ring on top and tipped the beef into the small saucepan he used for his camp cooking. Once it was heating, he dragged the swag off the back of the ute and set it up away from the house well away from the water. He wouldn't impose on them and he didn't want to get too friendly. He'd turn the conversation to them moving out after they'd eaten, then he'd hit the sack and leave at first light tomorrow.

Damn. He frowned as he looked around. It was too dark to have a good look at the site now and think about where to position the lodge and the jetty. He'd have to stay for a while after sunrise in the morning. But once he'd sorted the tenancy situation out tonight, there'd be no need to see Nicole again tomorrow. He'd reimburse her the rent from the day of settlement, and then follow it up with Foley back in Normanton.

He should have known the sale had gone too smoothly. Foley was the biggest scammer in the north.

The smell of aromatic herbs pulled him from his brooding, and he opened the packet of instant rice and stirred it in. After bringing the stew to the boil and a couple of minutes of letting it bubble, he turned the gas off, picked up the saucepan and headed for the stairs. Nicole had switched on most of the lights, and that surprised him, but he guessed she thought if there was anywhere around tonight he was here to deal with them.

He stared at the house. How the hell had she lived out here for over a year? If Binnie was going to be five, she'd have to go to school soon, so that was another persuasion he could use. A child that age needed stimulation from being with other kids.

Yeah, and you'd know, wouldn't you, he thought. Until Jenni and Jake's Leni had arrived a couple of years back, he'd had nothing to do with kids.

Ever.

The house looked less in need of renovation with the soft lights shining from the inside. It was a graceful old homestead, and he stood back and had a good look at it. The basic structure seemed good; the roof was rusty but maybe a coat of paint would fix that. It all depended if it leaked or not, but he could check those details with Nicole.

Before you evict her.

Dane took a deep breath and held the hot saucepan carefully as he crossed to the house yard and then climbed the steps. 'Dinner's ready,' he called out cheerfully as he tapped on the door with his free hand.

'It smells good.' The quiet voice came from a chair at the side of the verandah facing the water. He wondered how long she'd been sitting there watching him set up camp and cook.

'If you've got a couple of plates and two forks, we're set to go.'

Nicole reached behind her, and a light came on. The table where she was sitting had been laid with a plain white cloth. Dane smiled as he noticed the small jar filled with wildflowers in the centre. A plain glass carafe of cold water and two small glasses completed the setting.

'Very swish,' he said with a smile. 'I hope the food does it credit.'

'It smells good,' she said. 'Thanks for sharing your dinner. I hope it doesn't leave you hungry.'

'There's probably enough for leftovers tomorrow too.' He held the saucepan up. 'This is hot. Will I put it on the cloth?'

She laughed and shook her head. 'It's not a cloth, it's an old bed sheet. The table's old and it's covered with paint and lumps of clay, so I covered it up.' As Nicole pushed her chair back it caught on a loose board and Dane reached over to grab it while juggling the hot saucepan. She reached out at the same time, and their fingers brushed. He caught the chair, but she pulled her hand back swiftly as though she'd been burned.

'I'll get a couple of bowls. Have a seat.' Her voice was quiet as she headed for the door.

Dane waited until Nicole entered the house and then he pulled out the chair opposite hers. Sitting there gave him a view along the verandah towards the back of the house. As far as he could see in the dim light, the floorboards were in good condition, and there was no obvious rot in the timber. The little paint that was left on the verandah posts was faded and flaking off. The vertical slats beneath the railings were bare of paint and had weathered down to bare wood. He looked out to the west; considering the weather would come howling in from the Gulf, the exterior condition of the house wasn't too bad.

He wondered what the interior was like. Craning forward in his chair, he could see through the open door of the room at the end of the verandah. With a frown, he stared at the equipment that filled the space.

It looked like some sort of workroom and he wondered whether the equipment was Nicole's or if it had been there when she took up the lease. If that was the case technically it would belong to him. More junk to clear out.

The door to the house opened with a creak and he turned around. It was hanging off one hinge, one of the things that needed immediate attention, if he was to be a landlord for the short time she'd be there.

'Is there anything else that needs fixing?' he asked as she walked back to the table. 'As your landlord, however temporary, I'm happy to see to that, and anything else I can fix with a few tools.'

'There's no need,' she said with a gentle smile. 'It's fine. I would've done it myself, but I haven't got any tools.'

'I'll sort it in the morning. Has Bobby Foley been up to check on the place while you've been here?'

'I told him there was no need.' She put her head down and fiddled with the cutlery.

Dane gestured with his head towards the end of the verandah. 'Is he using it for storage?'

'No, that's mine,' she said slowly. There was silence and then she continued. 'It's an excellent space for me to work. That's another reason why this house suits us very well.' Her chin came up and determination filled her eyes as she held his gaze. 'I can keep an eye on Binnie while she plays, and when she's asleep I'm still within hearing range.'

'What sort of work do you do?'

The tip of her tongue appeared between pink lips as she stared at him. Pale blue eyes surrounded by blonde lashes narrowed and a frown wrinkled her brow.

Dane waved his hand. 'Sorry, I'm probably asking too many questions. I don't mean to pry.'

'It's all right. I'm a potter. It's not a secret.'

He was getting used to the soft gentle tones of her voice. 'What sort of things do you make?'

'All sorts of different pieces. But mainly large commissions.' She shrugged ruefully. 'That's the only problem with being out here. It's a bit hard to get the heavier pieces to the post office and freight them down to the city. Not to mention expensive.'

'I guess there would be quite a few things that would be hard about living out here.' Dane was still having trouble coming to the grips with the fact that Nicole and her little girl had lived out here for over a year. He'd seen many squatters and itinerants pass through in the years he'd worked on the waterways of the Gulf of Carpentaria. It was hard not to pigeonhole them into a stereotype, but they were usually a bit rough around the edges and most had attitude. Men and women.

Nicole had a gentleness to her. He could imagine her in a fancy restaurant or a flash house in a big city, not that he'd had a lot to do with either of them. She held herself gracefully and her movements were slow and considered.

Class.

That was what she had; she oozed class.

Now her slight shrug was hard to define as she held his gaze in the dim light. 'I like it out here. It suits me very well.'

'Well, it's not the time to talk about that. Let's eat while it's hot and then we can talk business afterwards.

'Let's.' Nicole nodded and reached for her fork. She lifted a forkful to her mouth and closed her eyes. 'This is absolutely delicious. You're a good cook.'

'Well, I could try and get brownie points, but I can't take the credit for cooking that stew, although I can barbeque a mean steak. As much as I hate to admit it, my mum cooked it for me.' To his surprise, heat ran up his neck and into his cheeks and he covered up his embarrassment with a chuckle. 'A bit like having my lunchbox packed.'

'You're very lucky,' she said. 'I don't have my parents anymore.'

She looked down at her meal and a wave of sympathy ran through Dane as she spoke quietly.

'Binnie is my only family these days,' she said quietly. 'That's why it doesn't matter that we live out here.'

'Well, I can think of several reasons why it does, but like I said we'll talk about it later. Let's not ruin the meal.' He picked up his fork and they ate quietly for a few moments.

Nicole reached for the carafe of water in the middle of the table and lifted her eyebrows at him as she held it up. He'd packed a couple of beers for the nights he was away but left them in the esky when he'd come over here. It just didn't seem right, fronting up with a beer in hand. It wasn't a social occasion.

'Yes, please,' he said.

'And don't worry,' she said with another one of those pretty smiles. 'I boil all the water out of the tank. The one time I climbed up and lifted the roof of the tank to check it, I was horrified.'

'Some wildlife?' He quirked an eyebrow as he kept his gaze on her face.

'Lots of wildlife! Luckily, we hadn't drunk any water before I checked. Now I always buy water when we go to town. But we've run out, so I am double boiling at the moment.'

'Do you shop in Normanton or Weipa?

'Normanton.'

'How often do you go to town?' he asked.

'About every eight weeks or so. Our food usually lasts that long and we've got pretty good at catching fish.' She looked past him towards the workroom. 'I've been trying to get some more work done to put in the Information Centre there, but I'll have to go to town before I get the last few finished. Supplies have run too low.' She turned her attention back to him and smiled, and his insides gave a funny little squirm. 'And thank you again for dinner. It's pretty good to be eating something apart from fish.'

'What sort do you catch?' he asked.

Nicole laughed, and the sweet sound rippled through the still evening air. The squirming in Dane's gut turned into a surge of warmth, as the happy expression stayed on her face. The wariness that had been there, to begin with had disappeared, and she seemed more comfortable with him being there. He found it hard to look away from her.

'I don't know the name of them. We just eat the same sort all the time. I was careful the first time we ate it, and when it didn't make us sick, we kept eating them. That's one thing up here, there's plenty of fish to catch.'

'Have you ever had troubles with crocodiles at the shore?'

She nodded. 'I've seen them up the beach a few hundred metres away, but I've never seen any near the house, but I'm really careful. Binnie gave me an awful fright today, opening the door. She'd never done that before.'

'Where is she now?' Dane asked.

'She went to sleep as soon as she'd eaten.' Nicole lifted her head and her eyes gleamed brightly in the dim light. 'It's been a very big day for her. I'll tell you why later.' She raised the glass to her lips and sipped the water.

Neither spoke for a while and the silence lengthened; it was obvious that she was searching around for something to say. Dane waited her out. She was going to be upset when he told her she was going to have to move out.

So,' she said finally. 'Tell me about your business. All fishing?'

'Yes, we have a family business based down in Second Chance Bay. My oldest brother manages it. Matt looks after the accounts and the fishing co-op side of things. My sister, Jenni, and her partner, Jake, have brought in a couple of new boats, and my other brother Don and his partner, have an exclusive charter business up in the Kimberley.'

'Wow, it sounds like a very big concern. What do you do?'

'I'm a simple fisherman. I take the charters out.' Dane put his glass down. 'My father started with a single prawning boat back in the eighties, as well as starting up the fishing co-op where we still sell the prawns at the Bay. We all grew up surrounded by fish and prawns.' He chuckled. 'And would you believe Jenni, my sister, hates fish?'

'I can.' She laughed with him. 'I can truly sympathise with that after only a year of living on it.'

'It's only been the last two or three years that we've diversified, and all of a sudden everybody seems to have their part of the business, so I decided it was time for me to find my own.' He gestured around. 'So, I bought this. I'm building a fishing lodge here. I'll be working with Jake and Jenni and bringing their charters here. But we'll talk about that later. You know all about me, so now tell me a little bit about you.'

Her face closed, and her lips set. 'There is nothing to tell,' she said. 'Binnie and I are living here. We are quite happy and I'm doing my pottery. End of story.'

Dane let that one go; he knew he'd overstepped the mark with his direct question.

'I have some fresh figs inside and I made some custard for Binnie's dinner if you'd like some dessert.'

'That sounds great, thank you. Can I help you clear the table?'

'No. You stay there. I'll take them in.' Nicole picked up the two empty bowls and the cutlery and walked inside. She was very finely built and if he was reading between the lines right, she was thin from not eating enough. There was not a lot of money to spare.

He was going to find out why she was here; if he was to have any chance of convincing her into moving, he needed to know what she was so scared of. Surely there were authorities to deal with this sort of thing, and refuges where they could be safe before women and children started a new life.

Hell, how could he suggest ways of helping Nicole when he knew so little about what services were available? One thing he did know after only a few hours; he wanted to help her, but he felt useless. His life revolved around boats and fishing. His awareness of social services was limited to what he'd seen on the television news.

Dane's thoughts whirred away, and he shrugged. His mother always told him he got too involved in caring about others. He'd always been the one who'd brought home the stray kittens and dogs, not to mention the new kids who'd turned up at school and had no friends.

So, he cared about the underdog. There was nothing wrong with that. People might think he was too interested in others' lives but that's the way he was, and it wasn't just curiosity.

The door opened, and Nicole walked out carefully holding a small chopping board covered with fresh figs. He jumped up and took it from her.

'Thank you. I'll just go and get the bowls and the custard.'

It was only a few seconds before she was out again. Her smile was wide as she sat down opposite him again. Dane got the impression that she was trying to be much more social too.

'Thanks again for the meal,' she said brightly. 'It was very tasty. You'll have to tell your mother what a good cook she is.

'Don't worry about that,' he said with a smile. 'Mum cooks at the local pub at Second Chance Bay and the nights that she's on, all the locals come out for dinner. Perhaps next time you come down to Normanton you could come up to the Bay.'

He sensed her withdrawal immediately.

'We go straight down and come straight back,' she said. There was silence again and this time it lasted longer. Eventually, Nicole passed him a bowl and gestured to the fruit and the custard.

'Thank you.'

They ate in silence, broken only by the clinking of the spoons on the bowls. When he'd finished, Dane pushed his plate to the centre of the table. 'Would you like me to help you wash up before we talk business?'

She lifted her head and stared at him. 'No, let's talk business now. I'll clean up after you go.'

Chapter 6

'Okay,' Dane said as she held his gaze steadily. 'I guess we need to talk about how long it will be before you can move out.'

Nicole swallowed and tried to stay calm. Their safety and their future depended on the outcome of this conversation; she had to convince him. 'I've paid rent and I have a lease.' She tried to keep her gaze steely, but her voice wavered.

'And *I* own the property and I have plans for it.' Despite his words, Dane's tone was conversational and held no threat. 'I'll do everything I can to help you find somewhere else,' he said kindly.

Nicole looked at him and she put her hands on the table with her palms facing up. She had to convince him to let them stay here. 'It's a very difficult situation for me. The bottom line is I can't afford to move. I have no money and until I get paid for the commission that I'm working on now, I simply can't move.'

'I'll go and see Bobby Foley and get your rent refunded. How would that be?'

'That would be a maybe. A very slight one,' she said slowly. 'But I'd rather stay here, for quite a few reasons. Surely I have some legal right if I've paid rent in advance and have a lease?'

'How long did you say you paid rent in advance?'

'Three years.'

'Wasn't that risky, giving him so much money? What if your plans changed?'

Her voice was bitter. 'Oh, there's no worry of that happening.'

'And how long have you been here already?'

'We've been here a year, so I'd need to be refunded two years before I could even consider moving.'

'I'll go and see him, and I'll get your two years' rent back.'

She nodded. 'That's fair. And then you keep it and I can stay here.'

'No, I'll give it back to you and you can move. I know a couple of rentals down at the Bay.'

Nicole shook her head. 'We won't be moving to a town.'

'Second Chance Bay is barely a town,' he said.

'No.' Her voice was fierce, and she saw the surprise flare in his eyes. 'Read my lips. We will *not* be moving.'

Dane leaned forward in his chair, and for a moment she thought he was going to reach out to her, but he ended up clasping his hands on the table. 'Okay. Let's be truthful here. If you want me to consider your reason for staying, you have to tell me why.'

She squeezed her eyes shut and shook her head. 'I can't talk about it.' Nicole was physically incapable of recounting "it". 'All I can tell you is that if we move there's a chance that our location will get out. Nobody can know that we're here. Nobody.' As much as she tried, she couldn't stop the trembling despair that broke her voice. She leaned forward and held her head between hands that wouldn't stop shaking. 'I don't want to talk about it. Please don't make me think about it.' She couldn't look at him. Her vision was starting to go silver at the edges.

'Oh no, you don't. Don't you go fainting on me again.' Gentle hands pressed the back of her neck and pushed her head down between her knees. A wave of nausea rose from her stomach, and she gagged.

'It's okay.' His voice was soft and gentle, and she took a deep shuddering breath as the urge to vomit passed. Her arms and legs were shaking, and despite the heat of the night, goosebumps pimpled her skin.

***

Nicole's reaction to his questioning left Dane startled. He knew her distress was genuine, and she wasn't putting it on.

'It's okay. Ssh.' He tried to soothe her by rubbing her back and the feel of her sharp shoulder blades beneath his hand was depressing. 'I won't make you do anything that puts you in danger. I promise. Please calm down. Okay?' He kept his voice low and even.

Gradually her trembling stopped, and she lifted her face. She was close enough that her breath warmed his cheek. He opened his arms as Nicole sat up straighter and she leaned into them. Her head fell onto his shoulder, and her deep shuddering breaths filled the quiet.

'Today was the first time Binnie spoke since it happened. It's the first time I've heard her little voice in twelve months.'

'It's okay, Nicole.' He pressed her head against his shoulder, wondering what had happened with Binnie, but reluctant to ask. 'You're safe.'

'That's how bad it was.' Another shuddering breath. 'He'll kill us if he knows where we are.'

'No one knows you're here. You're safe. I won't let anyone hurt you. Or Binnie.'

He felt her relax in his arms slightly.

'Thank you. It's the first time anyone has cared.' She shook her head and her hair brushed against his face. 'But not because they didn't care, because nobody knew.' The last word was a whisper.

'You look exhausted. Go inside and freshen up, and I'll make you a hot drink. And then I think you should go and get some sleep.' He kept his voice gentle. 'When you're in bed, I'll go down and get my swag and I'm going to sleep on the verandah. Is that okay?'

She nodded. 'Thank you.'

##

Dane woke with a start as the early morning bird song filled the air the next morning. Bits was still asleep snuggled up against his back. He had stayed awake most of the night, listening for any sound inside, but once Nicole had gone into the bedroom carrying the cup of tea he'd made, all had been quiet. He'd finally drifted off after four a.m.

He sat up and rubbed his hand over his chin. A shave and a shower were needed, but that would have to wait until he got home. Unzipping the swag, he climbed out. The pup followed him and ran down the stairs to the grass.

'Good boy.' He crossed to the edge of the verandah and gripped the railing, grimacing as the timber crumbled beneath his hand.

Hmm. What he'd feared

But that was the least of his worries this morning. He had to figure out what to do with Nicole, the tenant who looked like she had to stay in his house until her situation was sorted.

The door opened, and he swung around. Nicole stood there. She wore a pair of jeans, a close-fitting white T-shirt and a mutinous look on her face. 'What time are you leaving?'

He drew himself up to his full height and stretched. His T-shirt rode up his front and he tugged it down. Her gaze followed it and for a moment the determined look on her face wavered.

'Leaving?' he said. 'If you'll let me have a quick look inside the house, I'll be on my way.' He couldn't help himself. 'As long as you're okay for me to go?'

'Of course.' Her voice was clipped. 'I'm fine. We're fine. Just forget all that last night. I'm embarrassed. I lost control and it won't happen again.' She folded her arms across her chest. 'Give me five minutes and I'll take Binnie down to feed the chickens. You can have a look around while we're gone.'

Before he could reply, she turned, disappeared through the doorway and the door closed in his face.

Dane ran his hand through his hair. *Well, that went well*, he thought.

He rolled up his swag and pulled his boots on and took it back to the ute. The only thing he didn't have was the camp saucepan; he'd collect that when he had a look in the house.

He grimaced again; it felt a bit intrusive, looking through the house while Nicole wasn't there. Shaking his head, he talked sense to himself.

It's your house, and you still need to sort out this situation. Just because you have an unexpected tenant you don't want—even if she has a past that's damaged her—you've still got the lodge and the loan to consider.

He heard a door close as he loaded the ute and looked up.

Nicole and Binnie were heading along the shoreline to a small stand of trees.

With another shrug, he called to Bits and walked back up the stairs.

Chapter 7

Binnie was playing quietly on the verandah with a lump of clay that Nicole had taken from her workroom. She was sitting there making a small puppy, talking quietly as she played. Now that Binnie had spoken, it seemed that the dam had broken, and she'd been chatting to Nicole nonstop since they'd woken up this morning. It was the one thing that was helping Nicole to stay calm.

When they'd come back from the chook pen, Dane had been waiting on the verandah, the small pup in his large hands.

'Thank you. I've had a good look through. The house needs some work, but I don't think it's too bad. Thank you for letting me take a look.'

'Not a problem. It's your place, after all.' Her tone had been bland, and he'd shot her a curious look.

'I'll hit the road now,' he said.

'I'll just get your food container,' she said. He gave her another strange look and she wondered why. When she came back from the kitchen, he'd gone down the stairs and was waiting by the ute.

No matter what he said, she wasn't leaving. It was bad enough having to go into Normanton every couple of months. The problem was he owned the house.

How many years would they have to hide? How the hell could she spend the rest of her life like this?

There was only one answer. Until Bruno Spagnolo stopped looking for them. And she knew that would be never.

Nicole sighed as she walked down the stairs to say goodbye to Dane.

'Binnie, do you want to pat Bits before we go?' he'd asked with a smile that Nicole tried to ignore. Not only was Dane a kind and decent man, he was handsome, and when he smiled his face lit up. She wouldn't let her gaze linger on his strong shoulders and long legs.

Binnie ran happily down the stairs, with a loud, 'Oh, yes please!'

Nicole waited on the small landing where the stairway split into two and watched carefully. One thing that she had been worried about—and had watched for carefully each time they went into town—had been Binnie's response to men, but it appeared there was no problem. She waved goodbye to Dane and asked him to bring Bits back for another visit.

Maybe she'd blocked the memories as Nicole had tried so hard to do.

Unsuccessfully.

Nicole sometimes thought she needed to go to counselling, but that would open up a whole legal minefield. Because she'd never reported what she and Binnie had witnessed, she was probably liable in some way. Grief clogged her throat and she cursed Dane McDougal for visiting and putting her in this position. For bringing those memories to the surface again.

Binnie held the little pup to her chest and buried her face in the soft dark fur. 'Goodbye, little puppy,' she said quietly. Tears pricked at Nicole's eyes.

What was Binnie missing out on, being out here in the sticks by themselves?

Maybe it would just be easier, and better for them both, to pack up and go before Dane came back. Nicole bit her lip.

It would be if she had money. Plus, there was no way of moving the equipment that she'd gradually got into her workroom over the past year. She had to be strong and get through this. She'd survived before and found them a place to live. Until Binnie was due to go to school she'd hoped they could stay here.

That in itself was going to be a problem when birth certificates and legal documents were needed for enrolment. But that was a few months away; she'd cross that bridge when they came to it. Until then they would've been right if the house hadn't been sold.

She drew herself straight as the last whirls of dust blew away from the road and the sound of the ute disappeared. She'd nodded to him when he'd said goodbye and the concern in his eyes had almost weakened her resolve to be distant this morning.

Embarrassment flooded her at the thought of how she'd lost it last night. The memories had taken over and for a while, she thought she couldn't bear it. Being held in Dane's arms had provided a safe sanctuary she hadn't wanted to leave.

His warmth, his manly smell, and his strong arms, not to mention his kindness, had made being in his hold a very attractive place to be, but Nicole had forced herself to move away. Dane McDougal probably thought he'd arrived at the crazy house.

After she'd disappeared into her room with the cup of tea he'd made for her last night, she'd lain there for hours reliving the memories. Strangely it had strengthened her and when she'd woken up this morning it had been easy to remain distant and formal. Dane had obviously sensed her withdrawal, but he'd been kind as he'd said goodbye.

'I'll go and see Bobby Foley on the way back to the Bay,' he'd said. 'And I'll be in touch.' He hadn't said how that communication would occur; Nicole knew he'd have to come back but she pushed away the anticipation of seeing him again. 'We'll talk soon.'

With a nod, she waved one hand as he opened the car door and put the pup inside. She couldn't afford to get close to anyone. There was danger down the path. Her knuckles were white as she grabbed the timber railing; there was only one thing she could do. She had to get to work and make as many pieces as she could and get some more money together.

'Come on Binnie, we'll boil a couple of those eggs for breakfast.' Nicole waited until Binnie put the clay in the sun to bake and smothered a smile as she saw the three-legged dog. Once the eggs were on the stove she crossed to the workshop and picked up her purse.

She pulled out her business Mastercard and stared at it. There were ten thousand dollars in that account and the card had three months left on it before it expired.

The problem was, Bruno would be watching the transactions on her cards.

With a determined shake of her head, she held the card, ready to put it into the back of her purse. As she held it, she stared at the name on the card.

Nicoletta Spagnolo. That Nicole had never legally existed, but with his connections, Bruno had been able to get a card in the name he had given her.

Who was she these days?

Nicole Curtis, the woman hiding in her outback haven?

Nicoletta Spagnolo, the well-known potter?

Or the woman she was: Nicole Smyth—her birth name. The woman she'd lost sight of over the past three years, since that fateful day that her sister had met Bruno.

The day that their lives had changed forever.

The meeting that had resulted in the loss of her sister's life.

***

In the end, Dane didn't travel any further. He didn't go to Dinah's camp as he'd intended, and he didn't head to the small settlement of Kowanyama. His research trip had been hijacked, although he had scoped out the land and the house, and he knew it was suitable for the lodge he intended to build. Instead of visiting the two settlements that were easily accessible from the house on the coast, he was keen to get back and see Bobby Foley and sort out this rent situation. He should have known there'd be some sort of complication, dealing with that scammer. The locals said he'd rip off his own family if there was a quid to be had. Although that was the oldies in town who said that; Dane doubted that many of the young ones would even know what a quid was. He'd front Foley first, and if he had no joy there, maybe he'd go back to see the solicitor before heading to the Bay.

Nicole had been distant this morning, but he could understand why. It hadn't bothered him. Beneath her terse and quiet exterior, he'd sensed she was embarrassed about opening up to him, and even more so for collapsing into his arms last night. Even though she hadn't told him exactly what the problem was, the depth of her fear and distress was obvious. She'd opened up his protective streak and his money was on domestic violence; Dane couldn't understand how a man could hurt or threaten a woman and a young child.

He could just hear Mum now.

Another stray, Dane? But after he went back to the Bay, when he'd sorted out Foley, he was going to sit and have a good talk to Mum. Her advice was always spot on, and hopefully, she'd have some ideas, because he had none. The situation had to be dealt with, but sensitively. Nicole had said that Binnie hadn't talked for a year. What the hell were they hiding from?

He could still feel Nicole's slight body in his arms and remember the fresh soapy fragrance of her hair as she put her head on his shoulder. As he'd held her close he knew that he'd given her some measure of comfort, and by God, she'd needed it.

How could he possibly leave a woman and a young child out there on his property? But short of packing her up and taking her to town, he couldn't force her to leave and come to town with him. There were a few empty houses at the Bay; as the original settlers had aged and moved on few young people wanted to live on the side of a river where their house was only accessible by boat.

He frowned; not being able to afford the move didn't matter. The rents were cheap, and he could help her move. It was the fear that gripped Nicole when he'd discussed her moving that was the impediment.

Dane was itching to get his hands on Bobby Foley and he'd be threatening him with all sorts of breaches of tenancy law if he didn't refund her rent.

The road condition deteriorated as the corrugations deepened and he turned his attention to his driving. Frustration niggled as he had to slow his speed; he was keen to get back home and make a plan. He hit the audio button on the dashboard and waited for the music to distract him. None of it took his attention from the problem that was pressing on him, and he hadn't even thought about the house or the lodge. All he could think about was a beautiful sad woman who had touched his soul.

Chapter 8

Bobby Foley lived on the other side of Normanton, and Dane detoured around the town and turned into the old place where the Foleys had lived for the past twenty years. Rusted car bodies, overturned boats, tattered prawn nets and empty fishing crates littered the front yard, the long grass growing through the various rubbish.

Foley had had a go at everything over the years, from prawns to charter fishing, to selling real estate. It appeared his latest moneymaking scheme was being a landlord.

Dane slammed the door of the ute after he made sure that the window was down for fresh air for Bits who was asleep on the front seat. He stepped through the bits of rubbish, ran up the steps and pounded on the front door.

'Foley! Are you home?' he yelled as he pounded a second time.

Quiet. Silence. No movement.

Not even one of the dozen or more dogs that usually lounged around the yard were there to bark at him. Dane knocked again but there was still no answer. Finally, he gave up and walked back to the ute. As he opened the door a car backed out of the garage next door.

Old Harold Johnson stuck his head out of the car window. 'Foley's gone, mate.'

'What do you mean gone?' Dane walked over to the fence.

'He left town in a hurry last weekend.' The old man chuckled. 'I'm betting Bobby overstepped the mark just one too many times. There were a couple of big brawny blokes here looking for him after he left on Saturday.'

'Damn.' Dane stared at the house. 'Thanks, Harold.'

'The local cops are looking for him too, so I don't think he'll be back in a hurry. I hope he doesn't owe you money because you won't ever see it again.'

'No, nothing major, just one of his usual scams. Thanks, mate.' Dane lifted his hand and waved as he walked back to the ute.

He drove through Normanton looking at it through different eyes, wondering what it would be like to be Nicole, being in a tiny town and scared of being seen. She'd be much safer over at Second Chance Bay.

He drove past the Purple Pub and the replica of the world's largest recorded crocodile. Killed by a single shot in Normanton in the 1950s, the creature's nickname was Krys and measured in at more than eight-and-a-half-metres. A ripple of fear ran through Dane; all he could see was Nicole standing on the shore fishing as a croc lurked in the shallows. Or Binnie playing in the yard as one spotted her with dark beady eyes.

He thumped the steering wheel in frustration and Bits looked up at him and whimpered.

'Sorry, pup. We'll be home soon.'

The trip back to the coast was quick and he pulled up at the pub in less than an hour, hoping that it was a day for his mother to be there.

The chances of talking Nicole into moving to town were zero. 'Bloody hell,' he muttered. 'What are we going to do, Bits?' Mum's car was in the carpark around the back of the building, so he gathered Bits under his arm and headed for the back door of the pub.

'At least we'll both get a good lunch.'

***

After Binnie had eaten her breakfast, Nicole tidied up the kitchen. She'd gaped when she'd opened the camp fridge and seen the food containers stacked inside. For a moment she smiled; Dane McDougal was a kind man. But then, common sense kicked in; he wanted something from her.

'Come on, Binnie, you can play on the veranda. 'I've got some work to do, and then we'll have to go to town in a few days.'

Thanks to Dane's kind food donation, they could put the trip off and she would have enough time to finish the pieces for the gift shop.

But Dane being kind to her didn't mean she was going to trust him.

As well as being a kind man at first, Bruno Spagnolo had been charismatic. Laura had fallen under his spell and married him after a whirlwind three weeks. Nicole suspected that Bruno being happy to take two-year-old Binnie on too was the catalyst for her single-mother sister to fall in love with the older man.

But Nicole knew she was as much to blame as Laura. Bruno's charisma and his interest in her work, and his conviction that he could launch her on the Melbourne art scene, had sucked Nicole in too.

Even when he'd suggested—firmly—that she take Spagnolo as her artistic name—because of the connection he'd said— he had been so persuasive that she and Laura hadn't seen a problem with it. The only thing she drew the line at—much to his displeasure—was refusing to move into the nineteenth-century Italian renaissance mansion he owned at Malvern.

'But, *Bella,*' he'd argued, 'there are fifteen bedrooms and you will have your own wing. I will set up a studio for you. You will be company for my Laura and our Binnie'—Nicole had blinked at that— 'when I am away on business.' Bruno was always overseas on business although the nature of his business was a mystery to Laura.

It had taken over a year for the truth to begin to surface; strange comments overheard by Laura from some of the businessmen who Bruno hosted in their home raised suspicions. The gradual isolation of Laura and Binnie from their friends and their old life always had a logical reason given by Bruno.

His possessiveness of Nicole, as his protégée, became overwhelming, and the day that a very distressed Laura had called her to come over was the same day that Nicole had decided to go back to her name and break ties with her overbearing brother-in-law. But it had been a year when Nicoletta Spagnolo had hit the Melbourne art scene. Galleries, exhibitions and invitations into the closed ranks of the art world. She had decided to go back to using her name and had planned to tell Bruno that night.

If only they'd seen the truth earlier, she thought ruefully as she lifted her hands off the wet clay. She stood there and watched the wheel go

ANNIE SEATON

around and was surprised when a tear plopped on the table.

If they hadn't been so naïve, Laura would still be alive, and Nicole wouldn't be in hiding, fearing for her life and that of her niece. She wiped a hand covered with wet clay over her face. There was no point dwelling on what might have been.

She'd done her best, and they had to look forward to the future.

There was work to be done. She switched the kiln on to heat and tried to focus on the day ahead.

##

Three days passed, and Nicole knew she couldn't put the trip to town off any longer.

The food Dane had left had been delicious and much appreciated. Although seeing Binnie's excitement at homemade biscuits and cake had been depressing. Nicole realised what a plain diet they had survived on over the past year. They couldn't live on eggs and fish for the rest of the week, plus they were down to the last carton of milk. She worried about using the tank water for Binnie even though she boiled it twice.

If the water was off…

That's the last thing I need. Her greatest fear was that *she* would get sick and that Binnie would

88

be left here alone. No one would ever know; it was a horrifying thought that made Nicole's blood run cold. There wasn't even phone service for her to call for help. At least Dane McDougall knew they were living out here and now that made two: Mr Foley and Dane McDougall. *At least that was someone*, she thought. When she got a bit more money together she'd get one of those satellite cases that gave you phone service out in the wilderness. At the moment food was the priority, with nothing spare for luxuries.

'Come on, Bin, we're going to go to the shops today,' she said early on Friday morning.

Binnie jumped up and down with excitement. 'Can I get a new toy, Mummy? Can we go to the library?'

Guilt flooded thought Nicole. Binnie had missed out—and was still missing out—on the normal things that a small child should experience each day. Could she have handled this situation better? Should she have gone to the police?

No. Fleeing had been the only solution. Some of Bruno's "acquaintances" had been policemen. Others had been thugs and even worse, she knew that some of them had been criminals. To this day, she couldn't understand the attraction that Bruno had held for her and Laura.

'Can I find someone to play with in the town, Mummy?'

Even Binnie calling her Mummy made Nicole guilty. She'd figured it was safer when they were travelling if anyone they encountered thought that they were mother and daughter.

The biggest guilt trip of all was that she had never asked Binnie if she remembered what had happened. The longer she left it, the more Laura became a memory and one that she wasn't sharing with Binnie.

Surprisingly, Binnie had had no nightmares, and she had never mentioned the day they had left Laura at the mansion. It was as though Binnie had blocked out the memory, and if that made her happy, that was the best way to handle it. It was better than the alternative: that she remembered what they left behind them that afternoon. It was only the lack of speech that had been an indicator that she did have memories.

Since she had started talking five days ago, she hadn't stopped. It was as though the little girl was trying to make up for those lost months. Nicole jumped when Binnie tugged at her T-shirt.

'Can we go and visit Bits, the puppy, too?' she said softly. Nicole was amazed each day by Binnie's fluency and comprehension.

'Not this visit, but we might get you some new pencils and a colouring book.'

'And a toy dog for me to cuddle?'

'I think we could manage that. Come on, we'll go and pack the car, and then you can put your pretty dress on.'

Nicole sighed. That was something else to put on the list today; a trip to the op shop. Binnie was growing fast and needed new clothes. They had a lot to do, and it would be late by the time they got back.

Maybe, if they were quick, she should go up to Second Chance Bay to the fish co-op and see if she could see Dane. Maybe they *could* look at the houses there that he'd talked about. She didn't know if he actually worked there, or maybe was out on the boat. It wasn't worth the risk of driving all the way, and him not being there. She suspected that it was a fair drive up to the Bay from Normanton, and she couldn't afford to waste the fuel. Or spare the time.

Why did she want to see him anyway?

Because he was good to you, her conscience chimed in. *The least you can do is visit and say that you're okay and thank him for being so kind.*

No, they wouldn't be doing that, she said to herself.

Wait and see until you get there. Maybe. You'll get a good amount for the pottery bowls.

No!

The one thing that Nicole wouldn't admit to herself was that she couldn't forget being in his arms.

It took almost an hour to load the car. Nicole had carefully wrapped all the blue bowls with the swirl of water in the glaze in bubble wrap that she'd saved from the last trip. The woman at the Tourist Information Centre in Normanton had said that the bowls had been very popular and said that they would take as many as she could supply. The tourists loved them as they just had a small "Normanton, North Queensland" etched on the side of the swirl in fine print.

She had three dozen made so that should pay enough to let them do a good grocery shop and buy some things at the op shop. Hopefully, they might have a little toy dog and some colouring pencils there. Every dollar saved meant they could buy more food and stay away from town longer. Nicole glanced down at her purse wondering if she should risk using the card and draw some money out. Maybe just before Binnie went to school they could go somewhere far away from here and use an ATM, but anywhere in Queensland was too close to where they were. She didn't want Bruno Spagnolo to have any idea that she was in the north of the country.

If she knew somebody who lived in Western Australia or Tasmania she could post the card and get them to draw some money out and post it to her. She did have an old friend in Perth and her address was still in her purse. She shook her head.

It wasn't worth the risk.

'Come on, Bin, get your shoes on. We're going to town, sweetheart.'

Chapter 9

'Hi, Mum.' Dane leaned over and kissed his mother's cheek as he walked into the large commercial kitchen at the back of the pub on the point at Second Chance Bay. 'Rick working?'

'He went to help Donny with the boats for a while. He'll be back about ten. Jake said you went straight out on a late-booked charter as soon as you got back the other day. We weren't sure when you'd be back.' Helen crossed to the cool room and pulled out three heads of lettuce. 'Be a love and wash your hands and break these up for me. I'm running late with Rick gone. Then you can tell me all about your new place.'

'I haven't had a chance to get my head around what's happened, with Jake grabbing me as soon as I hit town.' Dane crossed to the sink and scrubbed his hands with the anti-bacterial wash. 'Yeah, there's a lot to tell.'

'Oh, no, don't tell me it was no good? I was worried about you buying it from Bobby; he's been no good since primary school. He used to steal our lollies way back then.'

Dane chuckled as he reached down to the stainless shell shelf for a colander and put the lettuce in and then turned the tap on. He leaned back against the workbench and folded his arms as his mother sliced tomatoes. 'Actually, the house is surprisingly good. There's just a slight complication.'

'What's wrong? Is it going to cost more than you thought to get it going?'

'No, the business side of things is all good. It's going to be a perfect location for a lodge. Have you ever been that far north, Mum?' He reached over and picked up a cherry tomato and popped it into his mouth.

Helen slapped his hand away as Dane reached for another tomato. 'Those lettuce are ready for your attention now. And no, I haven't been up there. So, what's the problem?'

Dane began to break the lettuce into leaves and put them into the bowl Helen had placed beside him. 'It's a beautiful old house, and I think with a bit of attention it could be a feature of the lodge. An old Queenslander in surprisingly good nick.'

He stared across at the large window that framed a view of the Gulf to the north. When Nicole had taken Binnie away from the house the day he'd left, he'd had a good look through, but it had been hard to focus on the things that he should have looked at. The more he'd walked through the rooms, the more he'd realised how tough they were doing it. It was like a monastery. The rooms were empty, apart from the two mattresses, the suitcases and the boxes he'd noticed when he'd carried Nicole into the bedroom. In the kitchen, there were two bowls, one frypan, and a small saucepan. He'd opened the cupboards to see if there was any water leaking in the kitchen, and they had all been empty. A plastic crate held a small amount of food and long-life milk, and he frowned.

Before he'd looked at the rest of the house he'd hurried out to the ute and taken everything he had out of his portable fridge and brought it inside. A strange feeling had lodged in his throat as he opened the fridge and filled it with the food. It had been almost empty.

Not sympathy, but more concern for the dire situation that Nicole and Binnie were living in and had been for more than a year.

'Dane?' Mum was staring at him with a frown on her face. 'What's wrong, love? You look worried.'

'I am,' he said. 'Someone is living in the house.'

'What? Bobby didn't own it?'

'Oh, yes, it was his to sell and now it's mine. There's no problem there. He just "forgot" to mention there was a tenant.'

'They'll have to move on then.' Helen picked up the knife and sliced the cucumbers at a speed that fascinated Dane.

He watched for a moment and then turned his attention back to the lettuce. 'It's not going to be that easy, Mum. It's a woman with a young child, and it broke my heart. They have very little food, and no money, but she refuses to move. She said she has a lease for almost another two years.

'Easy fixed. Bobby Foley will have to reimburse her rent and she'll have to move on.'

'That's the logical solution, but there are complications.'

Mum shook her head. 'Isn't there always with some of the people who come up here?'

'I think Nicole and her little girl are hiding from her husband. She was terrified when I said she'd have to leave. She was so upset when I asked her what had happened, she fainted.'

'Another stray for you to collect, son?' Helen walked over and put her hand on his shoulder. 'Did she tell you what happened?'

'No, she was very private, and I sensed when I left that she regretted telling me the little that she did.'

'You can't take it all on board, you know. There's many out there who need help.'

'I know, Mum. But I can't stop thinking about her.'

'The Dustan place is empty. She could move in there.'

'I suggested that, but she's adamant about not coming into a town. She's seriously frightened.'

'If it's that bad, surely the police could be involved? An AVO?'

'I don't know. She's got to come into town for supplies soon—although I left all the food I had for them—and I'll try and catch her then.' He put the last of the lettuce leaves in the bowl. 'She does pottery and she sells her pieces in Normanton. I saw some of her work when I was looking through the house. Dark blue pieces with a water pattern in them. She's very good.'

Helen looked at Dane for a moment and then crossed to the big cupboard where the plates and bowls were kept. She opened the door and pulled out a bowl.

Dane's eyes widened. 'That's one of Nicole's.'

'I bought a set last week when I was in Normanton. I use these for the individual salad. I'd like to meet her. I've asked Jill to see her about a set of speciality plates. Nicole Curtis, Jill at the shop said her name was.'

'That's her.'

'So, what are you thinking about doing?'

Dane ran his hand along the back of his neck. 'I don't know. It's hard. I'm keen to get work started there, but I also don't want to evict her. One thing she'd done there is set up a workroom with her equipment. But the other problem is the little girl. She's almost five and she'll have to go to school soon.'

'You need to go and see Bobby Foley and get her rent back.'

Dane huffed. 'Yeah, I tried that. He's left town.'

'Again,' Helen said dryly. 'He'll be back.'

'Yeah, maybe so, but that doesn't solve my problem.'

'I'd like to place a large order for here. I'm refurbishing the restaurant.'

'That's great. It would sure help Nicole money-wise.'

'I wouldn't be doing it out of charity, she's a very talented young lady. I remember seeing similar work at an exhibition in Melbourne when Rick and I were travelling, but I can't remember the potter's name.'

'Melbourne? I wonder?' Dane mused.

'Do you think it would help if I came with you next time and spoke to her? Reassured her and gave her some options?'

Dane shrugged. 'It's worth a try, I guess.'

'Okay, let me know when you're going up next and I'll roster myself off for a couple of days.'

Dane moved around the bench and hugged Helen. 'You know what, Mum?' he said with a smile. 'I think I know where I got my "looking after strays" habit from.'

'Get away with you, son.'

Dane picked up another tomato and popped it into his mouth as he left to go back to the co-op. He wanted to pick Matt's accountancy brains.

***

There hadn't been much rain since the last time they'd been to Normanton and the road was dry the whole way. The corrugations weren't too bad and there was no traffic on the track from the coast to the main road that joined Weipa and Normanton. Once they turned off the track onto the main road, Nicole's nerves kicked in. They were out in the world now, passing other cars and heading to a town of over one thousand residents. Still small, but there was always the possibility of seeing someone she knew.

And being recognised.

The main road was in worse condition than the track because of the constant traffic and trucks that chewed the road up. She glanced into the back seat of the Subaru to make sure that the box of pottery was strapped in securely. She smiled as she turned back to the road. Binnie was fast asleep, clutching the one tatty soft toy she owned.

The town was quiet and there was a space outside the Tourist Information Centre. Nicole parked and sat in the car for a few minutes getting her courage up. She looked up and down the street, but there was only an elderly couple walking away from where she'd parked. With a deep breath, she reached over and shook Binnie gently.

'We're here, sweetheart.'

Binnie waited on the footpath while Nicole carefully lifted the box out. She held on to the edge of Nicole's T-shirt as they walked into the building

'Oh, hello.' The woman greeted them. 'I was hoping you'd come back soon. I have some news for you.' Her smile was wide, but Nicole looked around nervously as she placed the box on the counter.

'News?' she asked hesitantly.

'Yes, not only have we sold out of your bowls, I have an order for you too.'

'Oh, thank you. Jill, isn't it?'

'Yes, Jill. That's me. Anyway, the manager at the pub at Second Chance Bay wants to order a set of speciality plates. If you're ever up that way, you could call in. I reckon you'd get a big order if Helen could meet with you. She's after a range with a fish on the plates.'

'Oh, that does sound interesting.'

'Can you do it? I can tell Helen, or if you could go and see her, I'd say it would be worth the drive.'

Nicole bit her lip. 'Actually, I'd already thought about going up there today. I have a …friend …up that way.'

'Where do you live?' Jill lifted the box off the counter and took out one of the wrapped bowls.

Nicole waved her hand casually. 'Oh, we move around a bit. At the moment, we're just visiting. We've moved down near Cloncurry, but we won't be there long.' She hated telling lies, but no one—apart from her previous and current landlord—knew where they lived.

'Must be hard to do your work, moving around.' Jill smiled as she unwrapped the bowl. 'Oh, Nicole, these are even prettier than the last ones.'

'Thank you. I was pleased with them too.'

'And the good news is, we put the prices up a little bit, so I can pay you a bit extra for both consignments.'

Nicole couldn't help her smile; the day was shaping up well.

'That's so kind of you.'

'We're a "not-for-profit" organisation. And we volunteer here at the centre. I'm pleased I was on today when you came in.'

'Is there a grocery store up at Second Chance Bay?' Nicole asked. She could do the shopping there and drive straight home after seeing the manager.

'Not in the Bay itself, but there is one at Karumba on the way in. It's a couple of kilometres from Second Chance Bay on this side of the river. Sometimes I go up there to shop myself. The fresh fruit and veggies come in on the boats at the wharf, and the groceries are a bit cheaper because they don't have road freight added.'

Nicole nodded. 'Decision made. I'll go up there, and I'll see Helen while we're there.'

Jill went to the till and pulled out an envelope. 'This is the extra money for the last delivery'—she peeled off some extra notes— 'and this is the payment for today's delivery. I'd be happy to see another order from you in another month or so if you're up this way again before you move.'

'Thank you, I hope I'll be able to drop in again.' Nicole shrugged. 'But who knows, my husband's work is itinerant, and we could move at the drop of a hat.'

'Well, I do hope to see you again.' Jill turned away as the door opened and another customer walked in.

Nicole swallowed as she put her head down and took Binnie's hand, clutching the notes and the envelope in the other. 'Bye, Jill.'

She hadn't handled that well. One minute she said she'd go up to Second Chance Bay, and the next she'd said that she may not be around due to her "husband's" work. But Jill hadn't appeared to see anything strange with her response.

She let out a happy sigh as they walked outside. 'Let's go shopping, sweetie. I think we can afford to buy you a brand-new toy today.'

Less than half an hour later, Nicole and Binnie were back in the car, with a new soft toy, some pencils and a bag full of clothes for Binnie. The little girl was holding the toy close to her chest; she'd insisted on the black dog, even though it hadn't been as pretty as the others.

'Bits the second,' she announced with a wide smile.

A surge of love hit Nicole squarely in the chest and she reached over to the back seat and squeezed Binnie's little hand. 'Bits the second, it is, sweetheart. You are such a good girl for … Mummy.' Her throat clogged and she swallowed.

The road from Normanton to Karumba was narrow, but to Nicole's relief, it was tarred. She'd filled up the car with petrol at a garage at Normanton and parted with two precious fifty-dollar notes. It was only an hour later as they approached Karumba and she drove through slowly looking for the grocery store so she could stop there on the way back after she'd seen the manager at the hotel at Second Chance Bay.

She found the small IGA supermarket and took note of where it was before she followed the signs to the next town. The shoreline was flat and identical to the coast up at her house. The Gulf stretched out in a silver sheen to the horizon, but here, unlike where they lived the water was dotted with many small fishing boats. A large container ship was making its way towards the river mouth.

It was a strange feeling seeing so much activity after their self-imposed solitude. Nicole followed the road until she reached the end. A small hotel with a blackboard sign at the front saying "Bistro Open" sat at the end of the road. Just before the driveway to the hotel, another road turned to the left and she slowed the car. The road followed the river inland. About a hundred metres along the riverside of the road was a building with **McDOUGAL'S FISH CO-OP** on the roof. A rush of excitement at seeing where Dane's business was based zinged through her blood, but she tried to ignore it. She was here to see the manager about work. If she happened to bump into him while she was here, so be it.

Who are you kidding? said the little voice on her shoulder.

Along the wharf between the hotel and the co-op, several boats were tied to mooring posts. She drove into the car park of the hotel and parked the car. She pushed her now full purse into the small handbag and swung it over her shoulder before she undid the seatbelt on Binnie's car seat.

Squaring her shoulders she walked across the bitumen with Binnie holding her hand and pushed the door of the hotel open. To her relief, it was almost empty. It was eleven o'clock and they were ahead of the lunch rush. A couple of older men sat at the end of the bar nursing beers, and low conversation came from the gambling alcove to the right.

The barman flashed her a welcoming smile. 'Morning. What can I do for you two lovely ladies? Lunch orders don't start until eleven thirty.'

Nicole smiled and bent down to Binnie. 'Would you like a special drink? A red one.'

Binnie nodded, and Nicole straightened and smiled at the barman. 'I'll have a small fire engine drink please.'

'And for you, love?'

She shook her head. 'I'm fine, thank you. I was hoping to see someone called Helen. She's the manager?'

The barman chuckled and shook his head. 'She'd like to be. And she thinks she is most of the time, but I'm the manager of the hotel.' He held out his hand across the bar. 'I'm Rick Curtin. Helen is my partner—in life and work. What can I do for you?'

A flush ran up her neck as she shook his hand. 'Ah, the lady at the Information Centre at Normanton said she was interested in some more of my plates.'

'Ah, so you're the mysterious potter.'

Nicole swallowed. 'Mysterious?'

'Helen's been trying to find out how to get in touch with you since she bought those bowls, but neither Mr Google nor the information centre staff could help. She'll be very pleased you've called in.'

'Is she here?'

'She'll be back very soon. She just went down to the co-op to get some prawns. Garlic prawns are on the menu today. You should try them. Her speciality.' He put his fingers to his mouth in an Italian gesture and a shiver ran down Nicole's back.

It reminded her of Bruno. She put her head down and spoke quietly. 'We'll take Binnie's drink outside and wait for her to come back. Thank you.'

He crossed to the post mix and mixed the drink quickly. With a flourish, he put an umbrella on the top and smiled over the bar at Binnie. 'One fire engine.'

Nicole went to get her purse out, but he shook his head. 'Don't worry about it, love. On the house. It's a business meeting after all.'

'Thank you.' She picked up the drink and took Binnie's hand, and they went outside. There was a large tree shading half of the lawn near the water, and they settled at one of the wooden tables. The garden area was deserted, the quiet only broken by the low throb of a motor as a small boat sped past on its way out to the fishing grounds.

Nicole drew in a deep breath of fresh air. Today, calm had descended upon her and the extra money from the Tourist Information Centre, and the possibility of another job had filled her with hope. Being in town wasn't spooking her as much as it had on previous visits, and Binnie was chattering away to her new toy in between slurping her drink through the straw.

Maybe she would go to the co-op and see if Dane was there. But what was the reason to go and see him? What would she say? Maybe another thanks for his visit? She should have thought to pack the food containers that he'd left. but they were sitting on the benchtop back at the house. Or maybe she could ask how he had gone with Bobby Foley?

Binnie was playing quietly with her new toy. Nicole sat and stared at the water and enjoyed the unfamiliar serenity until the dark thoughts crowded in.

Chapter 10

It had been one of those black days in Melbourne when you needed a scarf around your face, and knee-length boots to keep your feet dry and your legs warm. The sort of clothes that Nicole hadn't worn for a couple of years. They hadn't needed winter clothes in since they'd travelled north, and then settled on the Gulf. She could give Binnie's away; she'd well and truly grown out of them. She frowned; the op shop at Normanton wouldn't be interested in them, and besides, she didn't want to open any conversation about where she'd lived before. So, the old clothes would stay in the box.

The weather on the day that Laura had called her had been particularly bleak. At first, Nicole had considered not going over to her sister's house, but Laura's voice had held desperation and Nicole had detoured to the mansion on her way to the office where she was working as a temp between the pottery classes she ran at the local college.

Binnie had been crying in the background as Laura had begged her to come. 'Nikki, please, I need you. I'll tell you all about it when you get here.' So, Nicole jumped on the tram after ringing the office. That was the end of another temp job; not that she'd minded because she hated working on cold calls for the various companies that used the temp agency. It wouldn't be for much longer because her art was finally starting to make her a steady income, thanks to Bruno introducing her to the Melbourne art scene. Once she had fifteen thousand dollars in the bank, she was going to work full-time in the studio that he had hired for her. And she intended to pay back every cent that he had spent setting her up, despite his dismissal of her intention.

'*Bella*, it is for you. I have plenty of money,' he'd said constantly.

Laura's Prado was in the driveway and Nicole remembered that Laura had picked up a new kiln for her and it was still in the back. There was no sign of Bruno's car. Nicole had been relieved; even though her sister's husband had sponsored her career, she didn't like the way he operated. She didn't like the way he was gradually taking over their lives. Maybe it was okay for Laura; she'd married him, but the way he was trying to control Nicole's career was unnerving. He'd even told her last week that she was to leave the temporary job that she hated, but she had emphatically refused.

'How do you think it makes me look, Nicoletta?'

She squared her shoulders and stared at him. 'My name is Nicole, and my working has nothing to do with how you "look", Bruno.' Laura stood behind him shaking her head, with a worried look on her face, but Nicole had argued until Bruno had stormed out.

Laura had put her face in her hands and when she'd finally lifted her head, her voice trembled. 'You shouldn't have done that, Nikki. Binnie and I will pay for it.'

'Laura, if it's that bad, leave him. Come and live with me.'

Laura had simply shaken her head. 'I can't. You don't understand. But please, Nikki, please apologise to him when he comes back.'

So, to make it easier for Laura, she did.

And Bruno had been happy again.

Since he'd married her sister two years ago, Nicole had seen her sister's vitality drain away. She'd given up her career as a librarian at the university, and eventually, Laura stayed at home all day with a three-year-old child. Even though Binnie wasn't his child, Bruno didn't agree with daycare.

'A mother's place is with her child,' he said often. 'And we don't need that small salary that you get for all those hours. Nicole knew what salary Laura had been on as a graduate librarian, and it wasn't small by anyone's standards. Eventually, she'd given in and resigned from her position and was dependent on Bruno for money.

On that fateful morning when Nicole knocked at the door, there had been no answer. At first, she'd thought that Laura wasn't home, which was strange because she begged her to come over, and she rarely left the house.

And her car was in the driveway. Maybe she'd taken Binnie to the park for a walk?

She was about to turn around and head to the studio where she had some pieces waiting in her workroom for her attention when the door opened.

Laura reached out and grabbed her. 'Quickly. Come in.' Her sister's voice was full of urgency. Once they were inside, she burst into tears and Nicole grabbed her.

'Laura, what's the matter? Where's Binnie? Is she okay?'

'Yes, she's fine. For the time being.'

'What do you mean?' Nicole gripped Laura's hands, surprised by the level of her distress.

'I'm leaving him, Nikki. I can't stay. The things I found out, all those things that I suspected, they're all true. I married a criminal.' Her hands were shaking as tears rolled down her face. 'And not only a criminal. He's a murderer. I know it's true. I overheard a conversation and he knows that I did. I'm so scared. As soon as he went out, I packed the car, and I want you to drive. I'm too upset. I've got to get out of here.' She dug in her pocket and handed Nicole the car keys. 'You go and get Binnie while I get my handbag from my room. She's in that cardboard fort you built in her playroom. Poor little pet overheard our argument, and she scarpered in there. It's her safe place, I think. She'd been spending most of the day in there lately. There is no way Bruno is going to stay as her stepfather. I don't want her tainted by his world.'

Nicole looked at Laura; there was a small suitcase on the floor beside her. She put a shaking hand to her mouth. 'God, Laura. I can't believe it. Where are you going to go?'

'I don't know. I'll hide out somewhere for a while and then decide. I've been squirrelling some money away.'

'He's not going to let you go easily, you know.'

'I know, that's why we have to go now. Hurry, Bruno'll be back soon—' Laura stopped, and her eyes widened as she tipped her head to the side. 'Oh God, that's the garage door now. He's home already. Quickly, go and hide with Binnie. Keep her quiet. Bruno doesn't know she goes in there. As soon as he goes upstairs we'll leave.'

'He'll see your car's out there.'

'I'll tell him I got it out for you to borrow.'

'But will he see your suitcase in it?' Nicole's arms were covered with goosebumps, despite her thick jumper.

'I don't know. But at least he won't know you're here yet. Quickly, go and hide. Now.' Laura's whisper was ragged.

Nikki reached out and grabbed her sister and held her close for a few seconds. 'It'll be okay, Loz. I'll look after you. Don't worry, as soon as he's gone we'll leave.'

Every day that had passed since that morning, she had been thankful that she had hugged her baby sister before she'd gone into the playroom.

Chapter 11

'Hello. You must be Nicole.'

Nicole turned with a start; anyone could have walked up to them without her noticing as she'd relived the past; she had to be more vigilant. Thinking about that day had brought the crushing fear back.

She stood and held out her hand, not surprised to see it was shaking. 'Yes, I am. And you're Helen?'

'Yes, I am. Helen McDougal. I'm so pleased to finally meet you.'

Nicole's thoughts scattered. *McDougal?* Suddenly she remembered that Dane had talked about his mother cooking at the hotel; she hadn't given it another thought.

'I believe you met my son, Dane, a few days ago.'

'Yes. I did.' Her voice was flat. Who else had he told that she was here?

Helen must have read her mind. 'Don't worry, he's kept your presence in the house private. I only know about you because he told me about your pottery, and I asked about what he was going to do at the house. And I'd already bought the bowls and I put two and two together. And don't worry, Dane is very discreet. Sit down, I'll go and get us a drink.' She turned to Binnie. 'Would you like another drink, sweetheart? Rick said you had a fire engine before.'

Binnie turned wide eyes to Nicole.

'Would you like one?' Nicole asked.

The little head nodded vigorously. 'Yes please.'

'What about some lunch for both of you? Maybe some hot chips for your little girl, and I've just made a big pot of garlic sauce for garlic prawns?' Helen smiled. 'It was very convenient you being out here. I've left Rick peeling the prawns. That's one job I hate! I'd rather scrub a grill than peel them.'

'Thank you, but we won't have time. I still have to shop for our groceries, and I want to get back before dark. So just a quick chat.'

'I can have a meal ready in a few minutes,' Helen said persuasively. 'The sauce is ready. And it's on the house for a friend of Dane's.' No matter how much Nicole protested, Helen insisted, and she gave in eventually.

'Well, thank you. I appreciate it.' She looked at Binnie was a smile. 'And so will Binnie.'

'My pleasure.' Helen went to walk off and then turned. 'Dane is coming for lunch too. When I went to get the prawns and told him about the garlic sauce, he said he might wander over. He'll be very surprised to see you here.'

Nicole nodded. She didn't know what to say.

'Stay out here. I'll eat with you too. The crowd won't arrive for another hour.'

'Crowd?' Nicole's throat dried.

'Just the grey nomies from the caravan park. Today is the day I have the ten-dollar special on. It gets them in every week.'

'Oh.' Nicole searched around for a reason to leave but couldn't think of one. 'We'll have to be very quick though. We only have half an hour or so.'

'Well, I'll get cracking,' Helen said. 'We'll talk orders while we eat.'
***

'So you think your plans for this lodge will come off after being up there to look at it.' Matt leaned back in his desk chair and put his feet up on the corner of the desk.

'Yeah, it's going to be good. I need to talk to some builders here and at Weipa to figure out the best way to do it.' Dane respected Nicole's privacy; he wasn't going to share that she was up there with anyone other than Mum. 'But I do want to talk to you about the best way to set up the finances and the company before I start.'

Matt's face lit up. Finance was his speciality and Dane often wondered how bored his oldest brother got spending his days sitting in the office at the fish co-op. Maisie still ran the shop most days, but occasionally Matt would have to come out and serve. Dane couldn't have stood being stuck in a building day in and day out. Being on the water was his choice and he loved every minute of it. This new venture had fired him with excitement. Once he sorted out Nicole's situation, he could focus on the construction. And he wanted that to commence sooner rather than later.

Matt pulled a foolscap pad and pen over in front of him. 'Let's talk some figures. You're going to have a good running cash balance if you make this a luxury adventure trip and charge accordingly, so an offset loan is the way to go. So what—'

Dane's phone trilled, and he pulled it from his shirt pocket. 'Excuse me.' He frowned as he glanced at the screen. 'It's Mum.' He clicked the answer button. 'Hi, Mum, what's up? Do you need more prawns?' A smile spread across his face as he listened. 'Fabulous, I'm on my way. Don't let her leave.' He went to disconnect but Mum had more to say and he listened. 'Okay. I was coming there anyway. Got it.'

Matt looked at him curiously as he stood and pushed the chair in. 'Her?' he asked.

'A friend of mine is up at the pub for lunch. I'm going to go and catch up with her.'

'I'll come with you. I wouldn't mind a feed of Mum's garlic prawns. I can almost smell the sauce from here. I'll see if Maisie'll hang around for another half hour or so.'

Dane hesitated. 'Ah, do you mind if I go by myself? My friend is very shy.'

'Okay.' Matt looked surprised. 'Who is she, and where did you meet her? I've never seen you so keen to go and see someone.'

'Long story and one I can't share yet. I'll bring you back a feed of garlic prawns.'

Matt nodded and sat back behind the desk. 'I've probably got enough to do here anyway. Has Jake told you we've been talking about replacing this old shed with a modern building?'

Dane paused in the doorway. 'No, he didn't, but it's a great idea. We might even get Jenni helping out more if we get a new building.'

Matt laughed. 'You think?'

Dane shook his head. 'No, you're right. She still hates the smell of fish. Thanks, Matt, I owe you one. Gotta go. We'll have a beer tonight.' He took off without a backward glance and jumped in his ute to drive the hundred metres to the pub to save time. He was terrified that Nicole would leave before he got there. She was skittish enough to take off.

As he parked, he could see Nicole and Binnie sitting at the table where the family usually sat. He locked the ute and sauntered across the lawn.

'Well, hello, you pair. This is a nice surprise. Did you hear on the grapevine that Mum was cooking garlic prawns today?'

Nicole's cheeks had a slight flush on them as she looked up at him. Her voice was soft and gentle as always. 'Would you believe I forgot you said your mum was the cook here? I came up to see the manager about an order for some of my pottery, and she knew who I was.' She looked at him from beneath her lashes. 'And she knew where I was living.'

He looked down as a little hand tugged on his jeans. 'Where's Bits the first?'

Dane crouched down, his eyes at a level with Binnie's. 'Bits the first?'

She held up a black stuffed toy. 'This is Bits the second. He wants to meet his brother.'

'Well, I'm sorry.' Dane pointed across the river. 'See that white house over there with the dark roof?' Both Binnie and Nicole followed the direction of his finger. 'That's my house, and Bits the first'—he flashed a grin at Nicole and was pleased to get a smile in return— 'is asleep in his bed.'

'Can we go and see him, Mummy?'

Dane stood up as Nicole answered. 'No, sweetie. We won't have time. We have to do the grocery shopping and get home before dark.' She turned to Dane. 'Thank you for leaving us your leftover food. It meant I had time to finish my work and bring it down this trip.' Her eyes lit up as she held his, and small wrinkles fanned at the corner of her eyes as her smile grew. 'They took it all, and now your mother wants to buy some plates too.'

A surge of warmth centred in his chest as she held his gaze for a long time, and he found it impossible to look away. 'I think you'll find she wants more than plates. I think she's going to keep you busy.'

'That's what I like to be. Busy,' she said softly.

'Here comes lunch,' he said. 'I'd better go order mine.'

'No need, Dane,' Mum said with a smile. 'I saw you pull up and you have a large serve here on the tray. I hope it's okay, Nicole, I did some chips and chicken nuggets for Binnie.'

'Thank you. You're very kind.' Dane noticed the tremble in her voice and wondered how long it had been since she'd encountered kindness.

The plates were offloaded, and Binnie looked at her meal. 'My mummy used to cook me chicken nuggets when I was little.'

Dane was surprised to see the flush deepen on Nicole's cheeks, and she looked down quickly. 'Do you want tomato sauce, Bin?' she said, and her voice was husky.

'Yes, please. My other Mummy, I meant.' Binnie persisted. 'We loved chicken nuggets.'

His mother reached for the dish of sauce she had on the tray to cover the awkward silence that followed. Nicole was staring at the little girl with a look of horror on her face.

'Here you go, especially for you, Binnie,' Helen said before she turned to Nicole. 'Nicole, I have a big favour to ask you, and Dane, it impacts on you too.'

123

Nicole lifted her eyes to meet Helen's and Dane was surprised to see a sheen of tears in them. She blinked, and it disappeared, and he wondered if he'd imagined it.

'On me, Mum? he asked.

'Yes.' Helen shot an apologetic look at Nicole. 'I was planning on coming up your way with Dane, the next time he went up there to meet you and to talk to you about the order. I'd like a whole set done, and with the lunch rush about to start, I don't have time now.'

'So, what's the favour' Nicole asked quietly. Dane glanced at her left hand with interest as she caressed Binnie's back.

Strange. She hadn't stopped touching Binnie since the little girl had made the strange comment.

'I was hoping to persuade you to stay the afternoon and night at our house over at the Bay. It's private if you're worried about that. I know Matt's going down to Cloncurry to stay overnight, and we could talk at length, and do some designs.' She looked over at Dane. 'And I know that Dane would like to talk some business with you too.'

'That sounds like a plan,' he said. Nicole was staring at him, and her expression was hard to read. 'What do you think, Nicole?'

Chapter 12

Nicole didn't know what to say. Her newfound serenity had fled when Binnie had dropped the clanger about her "other" Mummy. Her stomach was still clenched, and she was just going through the motions of eating the meal, delicious as it was.

'I've got to go and put some more rice on,' Helen said. 'It looks like the bistro is about to get busy. Like I said, you're most welcome to stay at our place. Have a think about it and let me know in a while.'

'Is that where Bits the first lives?' Binnie said around a mouthful of chips, and Nicole's stomach muscles tightened even more. To Dane's credit, he didn't buy into the conversation. For the first time in a week, Nicole had the awful thought that it would have been better if Binnie hadn't been talking.

As the thought crossed her mind, guilt flooded through her and she came to a snap decision. 'I think we could manage that, especially if Bits will be there.' She turned to Dane and noted the surprise on his face. He'd expected her to decline the offer.

He nodded and smiled. 'Bits will be there, and I'm sure he'd love to see you again, Binnie.'

The little girl picked up another chip. 'Well, that's settled then,' she said with a nod.

Nicole's mouth dropped open, and her lips tilted in a half smile as she locked gazes with Dane. 'Where on earth does she pick up these expressions?'

He shrugged. 'Television?'

She shook her head. 'Binnie hasn't seen any television for a while.'

'Just a smart little button, then,' Dane said.

Nicole looked at Binnie thoughtfully. 'She's taken more on board over the past year than I realised. When she wasn't talking I'd have long conversations with her, and it looks like she was taking it all in.'

Helen came back and placed a carafe of water and some glasses on the table. 'I thought three red drinks might be a bit much.'

'Thank you,' Nicole said. 'And Helen? I'll accept your offer. Thank you. It'll be good for Binnie to have some company other than me too.'

Helen glanced at Dane and a look passed between them. 'I don't know how you'll feel about this, but my daughter has a little girl a bit younger than Binnie. How would you feel about Jenni and Leni coming over to the house this afternoon? The girls could play while we talk about the design I'd like you to try.'

Nicole bit her lip. 'You are all being extremely kind and thoughtful. I guess that would be fine. But,' —she looked around anxiously at the crowd beginning to drift out to the tables in the garden— 'is it okay if we leave now?'

Dane stood and gestured to her bowl. 'Would you like Mum to put that in a takeaway for you?'

Nicole put a hand on her stomach. 'Oh no, but thank you. I've had plenty. Binnie's finished too. Come on, Binnie, it's time to go.' She looked across at Helen and spoke quickly as she stood and grabbed Binnie's hand. 'Thank you for the meal, I'll see you later.' The more people who walked out of the pub, the deeper her anxiety grew. She picked up the toy from the end of the table, and took off, almost dragging the little girl to the car.

***

Dane raised his eyebrows at his mother before he followed Nicole to the car park. By the time he caught up to her, she had the little girl buckled into her car seat. She stood straight and closed the door, dragging in deep breaths.

127

'This was so not a good idea,' she said shakily. 'I need to go home.'

He couldn't help himself. Dane put his hands on her shoulders—thin frail shoulders—and held her gently, but firmly. 'I want you to take one slow deep breath, and then breathe it out. There's nothing to be afraid of.'

Her face changed in an instant. 'Nothing? What would you know about what I have to be scared of?'

His fingers still gripped her shoulders. 'Look around you, Nicole. We are the only ones in the car park, and no one within sight is paying us any attention. You're okay. Binnie's okay. You're safe.' Gradually her breathing evened out, and her shoulders relaxed beneath his hands. This time he held his breath as she lowered her forehead to his shoulder. 'It's just so hard. I don't know how much longer I can do this.'

He lowered his hands and laced them loosely around her waist and she didn't move away. 'Just stay calm. I'll keep you safe, I promise.'

And in that instant, Dane realised how much he meant that. This gentle woman and her little girl had touched something deep within him; a part of him that had never kicked in before. He cared about what happened to them; and not only that, he cared about how they felt. He wanted Nicole to be happy.

To smile and laugh and live life without being scared.

Gradually she pulled back and looked up at him. 'I'm okay now. Tell me where I have to go to get to this place of your Mum's.'

'Are you right to drive?'

'I am.'

'Then jump in and follow me. We haven't got far to go.' He winked at her and ran across to his ute. By the time he was inside and had it in reverse, she'd started the car and followed him when he drove out onto the road. Less than a hundred metres on, he swung into the vacant block beside the co-op and waited for Nicole to park beside him.

He expelled a sigh of relief as she did. Until the last moment, he'd still wondered whether she would follow him. He walked over to the car and stood by her open window. 'Anything you need tonight, or anything valuable, bring with you. It's usually fairly safe around here, but you never know.'

While she got Binnie out and filled a small bag from the car, he went down and checked the boat. He'd hate it to be the one that was always full of smelly crab and fish traps, but he was in luck. Matt had brought the newer one over this morning.

Binnie's eyes were wide as he led them down to the shore and helped them climb in. 'It's the only way we can get to Second Chance Bay,' he reassured Nicole. 'It's not a thriving metropolis.' She was quiet as they quickly crossed the river and he swung the boat into the jetty at the back of the house. Mum was going to call into the co-op and make sure Matt was still going to Cloncurry, so Nicole wasn't overwhelmed by too many members of the family turning up.

Jenni would come over after Leni had her afternoon sleep. He jumped out and looped the rope around the post and then held his hand out for the bag that Nicole clutched on her lap. At the same time, he reached down and put one arm beneath Binnie's legs and swung her out of the boat. Her giggle made him smile.

'You go and wait by the gate and call Bits and I'll help Mummy out.' Dane held out his hand. Nicole reached up and took it and he helped her out.

'Thank you,' she said dropping his hand as soon as she landed lightly on the timber jetty.

Binnie had already found Bits standing at the gate wagging his tail. She was on her tippy toes trying to reach over the gate. Dane scooped her up and lifted her over onto the newly-mown grass and she lay on the grass beside the pup chattering away.

He turned to Nicole. 'It's never the right thing to say to a lady, but you looked tired.'

'I must admit not having to do that drive back this afternoon is a relief. It's been a big day.' She stared at Binnie and spoke almost beneath her breath. 'An emotional day.'

'How about I show you the guest room, and make you a cup of tea, and you can have a rest. I'm happy to keep an eye on Binnie. Unless you want her to have a sleep too? Mum'll be over about three and you'll have a couple of hours before she goes back to cook tonight.'

'I don't think there's much chance of a sleep with Bits the first around.' She smiled, and he ignored that feeling that settled in his chest every time she did. 'I think Bits number two has been forgotten.

Dane looked down at her as she watched Binnie play with his pup. 'She's a good kid, Nicole. You've done a fine job with her, considering how you've been living by yourselves.'

'Thank you. Instead of me having a rest, put that cuppa on, and I'd like to talk to you about the house.'

He opened the back door and led her down the hall. 'Binnie will be fine in the backyard. It's fenced, and I locked the gate.'

He gestured to a chair next to the kitchen window where she could see Binnie playing with Bits. 'Tea or coffee?'

'Coffee, please. Instant is fine.'

He made the coffee and sat on the other chair near the window. At least since Mum and Rick had been home from their travels, she'd organised a woman to come in and keep the house tidy. When he and Donny and Matt had been living together last year, it had turned into a bit of a pigsty, and Mum had roasted them when they'd come home in the caravan.

'Did you see Bobby Foley about getting my rent back?' Nicole cut straight to the chase.

Dane shook his head. 'No. He's left town.'

She nodded briskly. 'Well, that's easy then. We stay there.'

'Whoa. Not so fast. I have a business to build up there. One of the reasons I wanted you to come to the Bay was to see how private it is living here.'

'No.' Her voice was quiet and despite the negative word, it held no nastiness. Just stubbornness.

'Okay. Consider this. Please.' Dane's frustration was growing at her refusal to consider an alternative. 'You're wanting to stay there because it's private and inaccessible, and you don't have to see anyone apart from when you come to town. Is that right?'

'It is. And I've paid three years' rent.'

'So how private is it going to be when I bring builders and tradesmen in to build the new cabins, and to do the house up.'

'I don't think you can do that without my permission.' Nicole's tone was sweet, but her gaze was like steel. 'I have a rental agreement, and I've paid my rent.'

'So, would you give me permission?'

Her voice was soft. 'I really can't answer that. I'd have to think about it.'

Dane bit back his growing frustration. He was caught between a rock and a hard place. He was keen to get his project started, but he was very aware of the fragility of this woman. And damn it, he'd worried about her non-stop since he'd left her at the beginning of the week 'So how long do you think you'll need to think about it?' He ran a hand through his hair. 'Look, Nicole, the last thing I want to do is make it hard for you. I guess from what I'm seeing you've had a pretty hard time, but you know you can't spend your entire life hiding in the wilderness.'

She lifted her chin. 'If I decide to it's my business and I can do whatever I see is best for Binnie and me.'

'But don't you think you might be seeing it from a narrow point of view? In the time you've been up there, your world has shrunk to the place that you live in. How many people do you see?'

She stared at him. 'None.'

'How many friends are you in contact with?'

'None.'

'What about family?' He kept his voice quiet as he sensed she was getting angry, but damn it he wanted to push her buttons to get a reaction. She was always so soft and gentle, it brought him undone. She must have the patience of a saint.

'Binnie is my family.' Her voice caught on the single word and she dropped her eyes. Dane felt like a heel and he thought carefully before he spoke again.

'What about Binnie's schooling? What about her interaction with other kids? With other adults?' He kept his tone conciliatory and patient.

Nicole lifted her head and her eyes were dark and bleak. 'You think I don't worry about that every day? You think I'm without feeling?'

'No.' Dane reached over and took her hand between his. Despite the warmth of the afternoon, her fingers were like ice. 'I think you are a very special person in a difficult situation. And I'm grateful that I picked Foley's place to buy and met you both. I want to help you, Nicole, and I hope that you'll let me—and my family—into your lives.'

He looked up from their clasped hands to see a solitary tear rolling down her cheek. Dane let go of her hand and stood and opened his arms. Nicole rose slowly and stepped into his embrace.

Chapter 13

Dane looked up as the front door opened just after three o'clock. His mother walked in carrying a thermal food bag, with Jenni and Leni close behind. He put his finger to his lips and pointed to Binnie and Bits who were curled up asleep on the sofa beside him.

'Ssh,' he whispered.

'Sweet little pet,' Helen said with a smile.

'She went to sleep watching *Sesame Street.*' He shook his head. 'Poor little mite was fascinated by the television. She kept walking up to it and putting her hands on the screen.'

'Where's Nicole?' Helen asked quietly.

'She was tired, so I offered to look after Binnie while she had a lie-down.'

Jenni stared at him, her expression one of amusement.

Dane stood and walked to the kitchen and they followed him down the hall. 'So what's that look for, little sister?'

Jenni shook her head. 'Is this my big brother here? You usually run a mile when there's kids around. And you offered to babysit? This must be some woman you've brought home.' She crossed to the biscuit jar and took out a biscuit and settled Leni on the floor.

'Keep your voice down, Jen. And I haven't brought anyone home. Nicole is here to have a meeting with Mum about her pottery.'

Jenni's response was between a snort and a laugh. 'Sure, she is. I can see the look on your face when you say her name.' She smiled. 'My brother has finally been hit with Cupid's arrow. About time! I'd given up on the three of you until Donny met Claire.'

'Jenni.' Dane's voice held a note of warning. 'Put a lid on it. Nicole's not travelling well, and I don't need you in here opening your big mouth and—'

'Stop it the pair of you,' Helen said quietly. 'Jenni, stop teasing your brother and Dane, you stop biting. Now I'm going to put the kettle on. Dane, you go and tap on the door and let Nicole know I'm here and then the two of you can take the girls and Bits for a walk while we talk about the set I want and see if she can make it for me.'

Dane did as he was told, and Jenni took Leni's hand and followed him out of the kitchen.

'Sorry,' she said quietly.

'It's okay, Jen. It's complicated, but it's not my story to tell. I'm pleased you came over. It'll be good for her little girl to have a playmate for a while.'

'Where do they live?'

Dane shook his head. 'If she wants you to know, Nicole will tell you. You go and introduce the girls while I get her.'

He walked to the room at the end of the hall. It had been Jenni's room when the family had all lived at home, and now it was the spare room for guests. Not that he and Matt ever had anyone stay since Mum had moved out with Rick, and Don had moved in with Claire. He tapped lightly on the door and waited.

There was sound of movement from within and the door opened. Nicole poked her head around it. She smoothed a hand over her tangled hair. Her cheeks were pink and flushed and had more colour than Dane had seen in them yet.

'Is your Mum here?' she asked quietly.

He nodded. 'She's in the kitchen. Did you have a bit of a rest?'

'I did. I went out like a light, thank you. What about Binnie? I hope she wasn't too much trouble.'

'The last I looked, she and Bits were both fast asleep on the sofa. My sister's in there now.'

'Thank you. I usually sleep lightly because I'm always listening out for her.'

Dane looked at her and it was hard not to reach out and touch her flushed cheek. Her eyes were heavy-lidded, and as he watched, she rolled her shoulders.

'I feel the best I've felt for ages.'

It was good to see her smile. He had to bite back the words that rose to his lips.

You look beautiful, he thought.

'That's good,' he said briskly instead. 'Come down to the kitchen when you're ready. Mum's put the kettle on. She's got a couple of hours, I'd say, so hopefully, you can get it all organised ready for you to go home tomorrow.'

As he turned to go, Nicole reached out and touched his arm. He looked down curiously, unused to the zing that fired his nerve endings at her touch.

'Thank you.' She lifted her hand, turned away and shut the door.

Dane was thoughtful as he walked back to the living room.

***

Why did I have to go and touch him, Nicole thought as she quickly washed her face in the bathroom adjacent to the bedroom. She ran her fingers through her hair; her hairbrush was in her handbag in the living room. Biting her lip, she stared at herself in the mirror. It was time to distance herself from Dane; it had been stupid to accept the offer of staying here overnight. She'd seen the look on his face; she was *not* going to become dependent on another man. It had been foolish to reach out and touch him; she didn't want to give him the wrong idea.

At least he was transparent; his motivation for helping her out was clear to her. The pair of them living on his property was the impediment to him following through with his business plan. At least Dane seemed upfront and honest.

Nicole had never figured out Bruno's motivation for getting so involved in her life; both professionally and personally. After he'd sponsored her as an artist, it was as though he thought he'd owned her. The doubling up of being his sister-in-law as well after he'd married Laura had seemed to cement that perception in his mind. Nicole knew she couldn't forget that, and she couldn't afford to let someone else try and control their lives.

No matter how much Dane McDougal—and his mother—wanted to help her, she would not let her guard down. No one ever did anything for no reason; there had to be something more there. They wanted something from her. She straightened her shoulders and headed for the kitchen. Maybe it was simply to have her move off his place, and maybe it was as simple as a set of dishes, but in her experience, nothing was ever simple.

Binnie's giggle reached her as she went down the hallway, and then Dane's deep tones and an unfamiliar voice. His sister, she guessed.

Way too many people getting to know them.

She bit her lip again; Nicole had intended being cool and distant when they talked about the order, but by the sound of the voices and laughter coming from the direction of the kitchen, it was going to be hard.

Why, oh why did I agree to this?

Because the money from this order will make a difference, common sense chimed in. *It will give you money to put aside for when you have to move on.*

And that day wasn't far off.

Nicole took a deep breath and walked down the hall and into the kitchen. A young woman with blonde hair was sitting at the table with a child on her lap, and Binnie was sitting on the chair beside them.

Helen looked on with a smile as Dane stacked a pile of plastic containers into a tower until a gentle nudge from Binnie had them all tumbling down to the table. Her little laugh was infectious, and Nicole couldn't help the smile that pulled at her lips. Dane had his back to her, and her gaze lingered on the muscles that rippled in his back as he lifted his arms to stack the containers again. He was a strong man, both inside and out, and held way too much appeal for her.

Be wary, she told herself.

'Fourteen, fifteen, sixteen . . .' Binnie counted, and Nicole raised her eyebrows in surprise.

Dane turned around as she stepped around the table. 'Binnie learned to count to twenty when *Sesame Street* was on before she had her nap.'

Nicole reached over and smoothed Binnie's hair back from her face. Her eyes were bright, her cheeks were rosy and there was a big smile on her face; so different to her normally serious little face.

Regret tugged at her. Binnie hadn't ever counted for Nicole, but she couldn't tell the two women it was because she hadn't spoken a word until ten days ago since they'd fled from Melbourne.

What sort of mother—carer—would that make her look like? As Dane had said before she'd gone for a sleep, what sort of life was she providing for Binnie?

A *safe* one, she thought to herself.

Helene interrupted her thoughts. 'Nicole, this is Jenni and my granddaughter, Leni.'

Nicole forced a friendly smile to her face. Her social skills were very rusty. 'Hello,' she said.

'Come on, girls. We'll go outside and play for a while.' Jenni looked hesitantly at her. 'If that's okay with you, Nicole?'

'That's fine. I'd like to get straight into talking business with your mother.' She knew her voice was cold; she didn't know how she felt about Binnie taking so easily to these strangers. If anything, a little seed of jealousy had sprouted and that made her feel awful.

'A cup of tea or a cold drink while we chat?' Helen asked.

'Stay there, I can look after myself,' Nicole said briefly. She crossed to the sink and picked up a tea bag and put it in one of the cups that were there. After pouring the hot water into the cup, she waited while Jenni led the two small girls to the door.

'You too, Uncle Dane. You can come and play, too.'

'Yes, Uncle Dane,' Binnie parrotted. 'I want you to come too.'

Uncle Dane! The jealousy grew another couple of tendrils.

'I'll see you in a while, Binnie. You be a good girl.' That was a silly thing to say. Binnie was always perfectly behaved, but the little girl barely glanced at her as she ran from the room.

143

Helen and Nicole were left sitting at the table.

'So, Helen.' Nicole picked up the teacup and tried to keep her tone business-like. 'Tell me exactly what you have in mind.'

Helen leaned back and smiled, and Nicole was struck by what a fine-looking woman she was for someone with four—that's how many Dane had mentioned, she thought —grown children. Her face was unlined, and her expression and her body language spoke of someone who was very content.

The older woman put her cup down and reached for the pencil and pad that was on the table beside her cup. 'Since Rick and I have been managing the hotel, we've tidied it up considerably, and business has improved. The restaurant has always done well, but we've started to build it up even more. We're going to expand the seating area outside, and Rick's going to put in a platform with a telescope to view the sunset.' Helen chuckled. 'After all, that's what most caravanners do the long trek up here for. The sunset and the prawns. Rick's looking after the outside improvements, and I've been tasked with making the restaurant more upmarket.'

'In what way?' Nicole asked, impressed by Helen's enthusiasm.

'We've already replaced the tables and chairs, and a new menu board is about to be delivered. I would like to have a dresser displaying your pottery, and I'd like to have a set of plates and bowls and platters all in the same colour and same design.' She gave a small chuckle. 'I don't know how hard it would be, but I had an idea for having a fish-shaped plate with the flat bit at the end in deep blues and greens.'

Nicole watched, impressed at the speed and quality of the drawing that Helen produced with the pencil. She nodded. 'Yes, I could do that.'

'Great. I wasn't sure if you'd have the equipment you need out there.' Helen looked at her curiously.

'It's taken me a while, and I had to get it delivered to the post office when I could afford it, but I'm fairly well set up now.' There was no point trying to hide it, Helen knew she was living out on the property that Dane now owned.

'And I guess that's one of the reasons you wouldn't be too keen on moving?'

'Yes.' Nicole's reply was non-committal.' If she and Binnie did move, she'd have to leave much of her equipment behind because it wouldn't fit into the Subaru. She wouldn't get a truck out there, because there would always be a paper trail to where she'd moved.

Now that she knew Dane, maybe if she did leave, he could store her extra gear somewhere.

Nicole shook her head. *No,* she wasn't going to depend on anyone.

Helen's voice softened. 'It must be hard living out there by yourself with a small child.'

Nicole lifted her chin. 'No. We do very well.'

'That's good then.' Helen obviously sensed that she didn't want a heart-to-heart or a shoulder to cry on. That suited Nicole just fine because she knew if she started to talk, she'd probably break down. She reached over for the pad and held out her hand for the pencil. 'May I?'

Helen nodded and passed the pencil over.

'Now how many of each would you like?'

The pen was poised above the pad, but there was silence from Helen. Nicole glanced over; the older woman was staring at her with sympathy in her eyes.

Nicole straightened her shoulders. Her nerves were already stretched tight and she didn't want sympathy that would push her over the edge. She was away from her comfort zone, Binnie was out of sight and with strangers, and all she wanted was to be at home in her haven in the wilderness. She looked down and began to make a list to give her something to focus on.

Plates.
Platters.
Bowls.

'I guess about a hundred plates and bowls, to begin with. And say a dozen platters. Is that too much for you?'

Nicole couldn't believe the numbers that Helen said. She'd be working day and night to fill the order, and she would have to get a lot more clay in, plus extra liquid glaze. Excitement curled in her stomach at the thought of the size of the order. It would keep her busy for at least three months with those quantities. And it would give them so much extra money for security.

'No, that's fine. I can manage those numbers.'

'I've got some magazines in my bag with some examples of what I like. I'll give them to you to take with you. Now you do me up a quote and give me your bank details and I'll pay a fifty percent deposit. I know you'll have to buy a lot of material.'

Nicole looked up and nodded. 'Thank you. I'll get the quote sorted tonight, and I'll give it to Dane to give to you later. But Helen'—her voice shook as she thought that this might be the death knell for the order— 'I only accept cash. Will that be a problem?'

Helen frowned for a moment and then shook her head. 'That's fine. I'll get around it.' She held out her hand. 'So, we have a deal?'

Nicole relaxed as she took Helen's hand and shook it. 'We do.'

Chapter 14

Helen and Jenni left together about five. Binnie and Leni had played together happily on the lawn as the adults sat outside watching the sun lower towards the water.

'I'll look forward to hearing from you, Nicole. I'm excited about this.' Helen passed the magazines over as they were leaving. 'I almost forgot these.'

Dane, Nicole and Binnie walked down to the jetty with them, and Binnie jumped up and down waving as Jenni steered the boat across the river.

'It would be hard to get used to, having to come home by boat,' Nicole said as the boat headed for the other side.

'In the wet season or at flood times, it can be challenging. There was a bridge years ago, but it washed away in a flood. The population over this side had dwindled so much, they figured it wasn't worth replacing it,' Dane said as they walked back towards the house. 'But we all grew up here, and Mum ran the household and the business singlehandedly after Dad died until Matt was old enough to take over.'

'How old were you when your Dad died?' she asked curiously.

'I'd started work, and Jenni had just finished high school.'

'That would have been hard for your mum.'

Dane shrugged. 'In some ways, it was easier for her. Dad wasn't an easy man to live with.' He reached down and swung Binnie up onto his shoulders. 'Let's race Mummy to the gate.'

Nicole walked slowly as they ran ahead, Binnie squealing and giggling. It made her smile, but it made her sad too. It was going to be hard for Binnie to go back to just her company, after the full day they'd had. It was hard to believe it was only this morning they'd set out. She frowned. As well as the grocery shopping, she still had to go to the library at Normanton to check her email. She'd order the extra clay and glaze online, ready to be picked up next time they came to town.

'Penny for them?' Dane's deep voice made her jump and she looked up. He was standing there holding the gate open for her.

'Sorry.' She picked up the pace. Binnie was running for the swing that hung from a large tree near the side fence. 'I was just thinking that I forgot to go to the library today.'

'You like to read?'

'I do, but it was to check my email, and now I'll have to place some orders too. For your mother's work. I said I'd do up a quote and give it to you.'

'You're very welcome to use my computer.'

Nicole smiled. 'That would be great if you're sure it's okay. It will save me time tomorrow.'

'How about Binnie helps me get some dinner ready while you do what you have to. There's a printer there too.'

'Thank you.'

Five minutes later, Nicole was set up at his desk. Dane had logged on for her, and she was ready to place her order. It was the only thing that worried her about ordering, but it would take a deep search by Bruno to find the address for the delivery of any goods she used PayPal to pay for.

She hoped.

As Nicole paused, the computer clicked onto the screensaver and she sat watching the photos that rolled across the screen. Many photos of Dane at various ages were interspersed in the collage of family snapshots. The other two boys looked like him, but Dane was the best-looking of the three. There was a photo of him hauling a huge fish into a boat, wearing a pair of board shorts. His chest was bare and bronzed and muscled.

She knew she was gaping, but Nicole's mouth dried, and she stared at the photograph until the next one rolled over.

Enough of that!

She opened Google and searched for a new supplier of the material she needed. She always used a different one so the order was a one-off. It didn't take long to find the products she needed; she ordered the quantities she'd worked out in her head and went to the shopping cart to finalise the payment. Her fingers slowed as she entered Nicole Curtis, care of Normanton Post Office, and then entered her PayPal account details.

A sick feeling lodged in her stomach. Every time she placed an order she worried that Bruno was watching. Maybe her faith in the privacy of information was naïve.

Once she'd placed the order, she quickly typed up a quotation for Helen and printed it out on the laser printer beside the computer.

Oh, how she'd missed the ease of technology at her fingertips.

The order complete, she turned back to Google and logged into her account.

There were three new emails, and she clicked on the inbox to open them. The first two were delivery notices for the last two orders that she had already collected from the post office and the third . . .

Oh my God. She drew in a sharp breath.

The third made her heart pound.

How dare he? Did he think she was a gullible fool?

Nicole stared at the screen until her vision blurred. There was no way on God's earth she was going to open that email. Her heart beat so hard that she put a hand to her chest and fought down the nausea that was clawing at her throat.

Bruno would know if she'd opened it. She'd used the "show this has been read notification" herself, and she knew that if she clicked on it, Bruno would know she was accessing her email

Her hands were shaking as she read the subject line one more time.

Please open this. It's Laura. I need to talk to you.

Nicole reached for the mouse to close the screen, her mind whirling and her heart pounding. It was as though Bruno was in the room with her and fear iced in her veins.

***

Binnie had lined up a row of frozen chips on the oven tray and was counting them as Dane prepared the meat that he had taken out to barbeque. His mother had dropped in a couple of salads and a small cheesecake, and he'd opened a dip and found some fresh crackers in the cupboard. He wasn't sure whether to offer Nicole a wine or not.

As he turned the oven on, he heard the study door close, followed by her footsteps on the wooden floorboards of the hallway.

'Here comes your Mum,' he said to Binnie, but she was focused on her task on the table. He remembered what she'd said about her "other" Mummy and wondered what she'd meant. Dane looked up as Nicole walked into the kitchen.

'Just about ready to cook,' he said as he turned around. He frowned; her face was pale, and her lips were colourless.

'Everything okay?' he asked casually, not wanting to make a fuss.

She nodded, and then shook her head and gestured to Binnie.

Dane nodded, understanding that she didn't want the little girl to see she was upset about something. 'How about a wine? I think you've earned one today, snaring such a good order. And a lemonade for this one to join in the celebration.'

Binnie looked up. 'Yes, please!'

Nicole nodded. 'That would be good.' A little bit of colour had come back into her cheeks, but her lips were still bloodless. 'Thank you.'

'A red or a white?' Dane crossed to the dresser and took out two of the good glasses that Mum had left here.

'Red please if we're having steak.' Nicole leaned over Binnie and ruffled her hair. 'I could hear you counting. You've learned a lot today.'

'Can we get a TV at our house, Mummy? I could learn lots of numbers.'

Nicole nodded. 'Maybe we can, but we'll have to buy DVDs because there won't be any television reception out there.'

Dane had picked a bottle of red off the wine rack near the door as she'd been talking to Binnie and opened it. 'You might be surprised, you know. There are some repeater towers all the way up the coast to Weipa and I know we often pick up television reception on the boat when we're up around Staaten River which isn't far from where you are.'

'Don't be silly,' Binnie said. 'Boats don't have television.'

'Oh. Yes, they do, Miss Big Ears.' Dane looked up and held Nicole's gaze as he answered the little girl. 'One day you can come on my boat and I'll show you. It has lots of things on it that will surprise you.'

'Tomorrow?' she asked hopefully.

Nicole dropped her eyes from his, and Dane turned his attention to pouring the wine. He couldn't get used to the feeling that ran through him when he looked into her eyes. It was a soppy, gooey feeling in his stomach, and he wasn't sure about it. All he knew was that he found her damn attractive and wanted to keep her safe. It would be good to see those shadows leave her eyes, and see those pretty lips tilted up in a smile more often.

'No, we have to go home tomorrow.' She lifted her eyes to meet Dane's again. 'But definitely another time.'

Good, that gave him a little bit of hope.

Hope for what, he wondered?

'Maybe I could give Binnie a quick shower while you cook the barbeque? We bought some new PJs for her today.'

'Sure. Just help yourselves. There are clean towels in the cupboard in the main bathroom. I've got some sausages to cook for Binnie. Is that okay?'

He was pleased to see that Nicole's colour had gone back to normal when she nodded.

'That's fine. And we do owe you for your hospitality and what you've done for us.'

Dane shrugged. 'I'd be cooking a barbie anyway, and Mum would have sent the salads over, so it's no extra work. Besides, I've got a few days between charters, and it gives me something to do. Not to mention good company.'

She smiled that gentle smile that sent his gut all warm and tight as she took Binnie's hand and led her to the bathroom.

##

An hour and a half later, Binnie was tucked up in bed in the guest room, and Dane and Nicole were sitting out on the back porch watching the river change colour as the night closed in. There was a myriad of coloured lights blinking out in the Gulf tonight; Dane was surprised to see the number of fishing boats that were still out there. The small boats, referred to by the locals as the "mosquito fleet" usually came in with their catch before sunset. But it was a pleasant night, the air was warm and there was no wind, and he assumed the fish must be biting.

Nicole had been quiet during dinner, but Binnie had chattered nonstop as they'd eaten the steak and sausages that he'd cooked on the outside grill. She'd sat back and listened as he'd answered the myriad of questions that Binnie posed to him, and he had to remember that it was only a short while ago that she'd started to talk again, according to what Nicole had said the night he'd stayed at the house with them. That had never been mentioned again, nor was there a mention of the "other Mummy" comment.

For the first time, he wondered whether Nicole had done something wrong, but the thought was fleeting. He knew instinctively that she was a good person, and he trusted his judgement.

'Would you like another glass of wine?' He held up the bottle and she jumped when he spoke. Her brow was furrowed, and she was staring into the growing darkness.

She nodded and held her glass out.

'You look like you've got the weight of the world on your shoulders,' he said as he poured the wine.

Nicole held the glass up and the ruby red liquid caught the light of the citronella candle he'd put on the table to chase the mosquitos away. A gentle sigh puffed from her lips, but she didn't answer.

'A problem shared is a problem halved, they say,' he said quietly.

She stared at him and her eyes glittered. 'You know, Dane, if you thought I was emotionally unstable, I could understand why.'

'I don't think that at all, Nicole. I know you wouldn't be living up the coast with Binnie unless

158

you had a very good reason. I know a lot of women live in fear from problems with relationships.' He leaned forward and took her hand. 'Domestic violence can be dealt with. You've taken the first step and taken yourself away from the situation, now you need to get help to deal with it. No matter what the circumstances were, you didn't deserve it.'

The laugh that came from her lips was like nothing he'd heard before; it was full of bitterness. 'If only it was that simple. I have to stay strong for Binnie and I have to be brave.'

'Did something happen this afternoon? When you were on the computer?'

Nicole nodded. 'I can't talk about it. I shouldn't even be here with your family.' She waved a hand and a few drops of wine spilled onto her lap, but she didn't notice. 'The more people that know who we are and where we are, the more chance there is of us being found.' Her voice was harsh. 'And that can't happen. Ever.' Her eyes were bleak as she stared at him. 'I wish you'd never bought that house.'

'But I did, and I'm here with you. And by God, Nicole, I want to help you. I want to make sure that you and Binnie are safe.'

She jumped to her feet and the glass of wine went flying. 'You can't help us, Dane. No one can.'

Nicole hurried across the lawn to the gate, her movements jerky and every line of her body tense. Her breath was loud as she drew in deep ragged breaths. Dane walked over slowly not wanting to spook her. As he drew closer, he could see her body trembling, and he put his hands gently on her shoulders.

'Nicole. Please. You can trust me. Let me help you.' Her frail shoulders were rigid under his touch until she sagged beneath his hands and he caught her before she fell. She turned and buried her face in his T-shirt.

Dane knew in that moment that he would do anything to protect this woman.

Once she started talking, she relaxed into him and the words flowed.

He held her close as his horror grew.

Chapter 15

Over in the corner behind the fancy dolls' house and expensive toys that Bruno had insisted on buying for his stepdaughter was a small fort made from old cardboard boxes. Nicole had made it for Binnie one day when she'd been babysitting, and the little girl loved it. They had painted it grey and looped a string of flags made from coloured paper around the cut-out turrets. The door was a piece of cardboard that had been cut from the side of a box and taped to the doorway that Nicole had made just big enough for her to crawl through and follow Binnie into the little castle. Small slits were cut in the cardboard at Binnie's eye level, so she could see out. Her little niece loved playing in it and every time Nicole came to visit, Binnie insisted on sitting in there and listening to the fairy stories that Nicole made up for her.

Laura had told her on the phone last week that Binnie had even taken to having her afternoon naps in there.

The sound of the door opening and Bruno's loud voice had Nicole scurrying across the room. She got down to her knees and crawled through the small opening, and pulled the cardboard door shut behind her. Binnie was sitting in there and she opened her little mouth wide to say hello, but Nikki put her finger to her lips and shook her head and whispered a very quiet 'shush' next to her ear.

'Laura!' Bruno's loud voice came through the closed playroom door. 'What do you think you're doing?'

Laura's response was quiet, and Nicole couldn't make out the words. She reached out her arms to her niece and the little girl snuggled into them and hid her face in Nicole's chest as the shouting got louder. Binnie's body was stiff, and Nicole rubbed her hand over her back in soothing circles. The little girl had heard this before; Laura had told Nicole that Binnie was crying in her sleep and had begun to wet the bed at night.

'Tell me where you were going.' More yelling came from the family room and Nicole closed her eyes wishing that the little girl didn't have to hear the angry words. The sooner they got out of here the better.

'You bitch, how dare you accuse me. You have no idea what you're talking about, you stupid woman.' There was the sound of a slap and Nicole tensed as Laura screamed.

There was silence and she held her breath until the soft tones of Laura's voice came through the closed door.

'Where's the kid?' Bruno yelled.

Finally, Laura yelled loudly, and Nicole knew it was for her benefit. 'Stop yelling, Bruno. She's up in her room asleep. You'll wake her.'

'Don't you yell at me, you bitch.' Another slap. 'Why is your car outside? Where do you think you're going?'

More muffled words.

'Nicoletta? Why does she need your car? I offered to buy her one, but she is another stupid woman. What is it with your family?'

The sound of loud footsteps came through the closed door, and then a dragging sound followed by a crash.

'I'm not a fool. Where do you think you were going?'

'I wasn't going anywhere. The suitcase has old clothes that Nikki was going to take away for me. You are so generous, Binnie has too many. I thought they could go to one of the charities.'

A slap and another scream. Tears began to roll down Nicole's cheeks as she heard her sister begging. She pressed Binnie closer to her chest.

'No, Bruno. Don't hurt me.'

Binnie's little body was shaking in her arms and Nicole moved her hands over the little girl's ears.

'You're lying to me again, Laura. You were leaving me. I won't let you leave. Why is your suitcase in your car? Do you have too many clothes too, lying bitch?'

Laura's scream turned Nicole's blood to ice. 'Don't touch me. No! Don't touch me.'

Binnie started to whimper, and Nicole let her go for a minute. She held the little girl's gaze and put her finger to her lips. 'We have to be very, very quiet and then we will go and help Mummy. Okay?'

Nicole pulled her close and put her hands over Binnie's ears again as the yelling intensified; she was terrified that Binnie would start crying, and he would know that Laura was lying. But Bruno was yelling, Laura was screaming, and Binnie stayed silent.

'No, no no! My baby. Think of my baby!'

Her last scream made Nicole's blood run cold and she fought the faintness that threatened. She had to protect Binnie, whatever happened.

A shot rang out in the next room, and there was a loud thump.

Nicole's vision pricked with white lights, but she fought it as she held Binnie to her. Bile rose in her throat and burned as she swallowed it down.

The silence from the room beside them was more frightening than the yelling that had preceded it. Binnie was silent and stiff in her arms.

The door opened, and Nicole froze. She closed her eyes and held her breath; there was no sound for a few seconds. Binnie was stiff in her arms and didn't make a sound.

After a moment the door closed again, and the footsteps receded.

Time ceased to have any meaning, and Nicole didn't know how long she sat there gripping Binnie to her. When she looked down, Binnie's eyes were closed, and her breathing was even. She'd found her release in sleep.

Nicole reached into her pocket and pulled out her phone and dialled the first two zeros of triple zero ready to push the last one if she needed to call emergency.

The garage door opened and there was a squealing of tyres and the throbbing tones of Bruno's sports car as he backed out of the driveway.

In the months afterwards, Nicole realised that she had known what she would find in that room. Somehow, she crawled out of the fort, clutching Binnie to her chest and the little girl stayed asleep. Slowly and quietly, Nicole crossed the room, opened the door and stepped into the living room.

The shock of seeing Laura, her only sister, her only family, lying on her back on the floor in a pool of blood, her eyes wide open, was a sight that she would never forget as long as she lived.

She held Binnie with her face pressed tight to her chest and ran over to Laura and bent down. One side of her sister's face was covered with blood. With shaking hands, she pressed her fingers to the side of Laura's throat, feeling for a pulse.

Nicole let out an anguished cry and Binnie woke up and began to scream. She tried to shield the little girl, but her scream rang around the room. 'Mummy, Mummy. I want Mummy.'

As Nicole pressed the third zero, those words were the last words Binnie spoke until the day Dane McDougall came into their lives.

Chapter 16

Dane's arms held her close and Nicole felt safe for the first time in many months. She gripped the sleeves of his soft T-shirt and kept talking.

'I strapped Binnie into Laura's car and we drove for six hours. I stopped in a small country town across the border, filled up the car and went to the ATM. I drew out as much money as I could. I did that for the next few days until I realised that it was giving Bruno a trail of where we were going. I started to pay cash for everything, and I didn't draw any money out again.'

His chest vibrated against her cheek as he finally spoke. 'What about the police? Did you go to the police at all?'

She shook her head. 'There was no point. I knew what Laura had told me over those past few weeks. She married a criminal. Bruno was involved in the gang warfare in Melbourne and she said he bragged that half the police force was on his payroll. He would have known very quickly that I must have been in the house and that I knew that he . . . I knew what he did to Laura.'

167

'And you think he's been looking for you ever since?'

'Of course, he has. Binnie and I could send him to jail if we went to the police. But I never knew who he had in his pocket. So, it was safer to leave.'

She stepped back and looked up at Dane and the expression in his eyes rocked her to the core. 'You . . . you believe me?'

'Of course, I do. I've seen your fear, and I've seen your strength. You are one amazing woman to have carried that with you … for how long?'

'Fourteen months.'

He gathered her close in his arms again, and she rested her head on his strong shoulder. 'What happened today to upset you?' he asked quietly.

'He emailed me. He pretended to be Laura.' Her voice hitched on a sob. 'My dead sister. That's the sort of bastard he is.'

Dane took a deep breath. 'I want to help you through this. I want to help you get back into living a real life. Not hiding out.'

'Why would you want to do that?' Nicole bit her lip. 'I'm sorry. Since Bruno, I don't trust very well. He sucked in both Laura and me; he took over my life as much as he could. It was as though he got glory from my exhibitions. He even made me change my name to his; he convinced me it would open doors. He was probably paying for those doors to be opened and I fell for it.'

'Will you trust me? How can I convince you that I mean you no harm and that I don't want anything from you?'

'Not even your house and land that we're stopping you develop?'

'That's the last of my worries at the moment, Nicole. I'm going to track this bastard down, and we'll make sure that he gets what he deserves. If you won't let me do it for you, let me do it for Binnie.'

She was quiet for a moment as she thought of what this man was offering.

Finally, Nicole stood on her toes and rested her cheek against Dane's. 'Thank you, she whispered.

##

After they crossed the river the next morning, Dane insisted on following Nicole's Subaru in his ute. Not only into Second Chance Bay where he helped her do the grocery shopping, but then he followed her the eighty kilometres back to Normanton. To her shock, he'd then insisted on following her car for the whole six-hour journey until they arrived in a convoy back at the house on the Gulf.

'You don't have to follow us,' she'd protested as they'd sat at his kitchen table eating breakfast, with Binnie happily drawing between them. A couple of times their gazes had connected, and Nicole had dropped hers. Something had changed between them; after sharing her story with him last night, she felt very close to Dane.

And she felt lighter.

For the first time, she began to think that maybe there was a way out of this horrid situation that she had been trapped in for more than a year.

He'd simply smiled and nodded. 'Yes, I do.'

But his decision to accompany her on the journey home had been made after she'd refused point blank to look at the vacant house a few houses along from his place. 'Not yet, Dane. Maybe one day, but I'm not ready yet.'

He'd listened, but then he'd insisted on doing the trip with them.

'Haven't you got to work?' she asked.

'Not for another two days.'

In the end, she'd given in, but it had been good to know he was travelling along behind them all the way. Binnie had kept twisting around in her car seat and had given a running commentary on how close Dane was to them for most of the trip until she fell asleep just before they turned off the main road.

170

Their house and the surroundings were deserted—as they should be. Dane parked behind them and came across to the car. He opened the back door and smiled as he looked in at Binnie.

'Do you want me to lift her out while you open up the house?' he whispered.

'Yes please.' Heat ran up Nicole's neck as she preceded him up the stairs. It was a very domestic situation. She unlocked the door, and Dane took Binnie over to the mattress on the floor and gently laid her down before pulling the light cotton sheet up over her.

A strange feeling ran through Nicole as he brushed his fingers lightly over Binnie's rosy cheek before he stood up and walked back to the door where she was standing.

'Come and I'll help you unload those groceries,' he said. 'And then I'd love a cup of tea.'

She smiled. 'I'll put the kettle on before we start.'

It didn't take long to unpack the car. As she began to put the food into the cupboards Nicole frowned and put her hands on her hips. 'I didn't buy these chocolate biscuits, or muesli bars or a block of chocolate.'

'My treat.'

'You didn't have to do that, Dane,' she protested.

'I just wanted to make sure you had some good stuff to eat when I call in next week.'

'Next week? You don't have to do that.' Despite her words, the thought that he'd be back soon made her happy.

'I'll be coming by sea. We've got a three-day charter up here.'

'But you won't bring anyone ashore with you, will you?' Her eyes widened at the thought of strangers coming ashore.

'No. I won't. We'll moor around at the mouth of the river where the fishing is, and I'll come around in the tender'.

'Won't you be needed?'

He grinned, and the flash of white teeth in his tanned face and the sparkle in his eyes sent a shaky feeling right through Nicole.

'I'm the skipper. The deckies can cope for a couple of hours without me.'

She nodded. 'Ah. I know nothing about boats.'

'We'll have to remedy that, won't we?' There was a promise in his words and the trembling crept lower, down between her thighs.

'Maybe.'

'That's better than a no.' His grin got wider. 'When do you think your order will arrive at the post office? I was thinking I could collect it for you, to save you a trip down.'

Nicole shrugged as she put the last of the groceries in the cupboard. The camping fridge was full too. 'I haven't used that supplier before, so I don't know. The post office has been good. They know I'm out of town—but they think I'm down on the Cloncurry road—and they hold my deliveries until I get into town to pick them up.'

'How the heck did you get all of that equipment up into your workroom?' He gestured to the room along the verandah.

She chuckled. 'With a lot of improvising. I pulled the kiln up with a couple of ropes; the rest I managed to carry up the steps and push along the verandah.'

'You amaze me.'

Nicole looked up and their eyes met and held. She looked down as Dane's hand reached for hers and he pulled her slowly towards him.

She didn't—couldn't—resist.

Her gaze stayed on their joined hands and her heart rate kicked up a notch as his other hand slid around her waist. Heat warmed her cheeks as his head lowered to hers and his breath whispered on her cheek.

'I'm going to look after you, Nicole. And not because I think it's the right thing to do. It's

173

because I want to spend more time with you. Get to know the *real* you, the happy vibrant woman who is behind this fear that you carry with you.' The warmth of his lips touched her cheek. 'What do you think of that?'

She couldn't think. Her brain had gone to mush along with the rest of her body. And then his lips slid along her cheek to the corner of her mouth. Butterflies were running rampant in her stomach and sending exquisite quivers down lower.

'You're not playing fair,' she murmured.

'I'm just thankful that there's a little girl asleep in your bed, or I'd be playing a lot harder. This is a promise, Nic.' His lips closed on hers, and warm liquid sensation flooded through her as she joined him in the moment.

She lifted her arms and put her hands at the back of his neck, pulling his head down harder. The kiss deepened as his tongue played along her lips, and she opened her mouth to welcome him in.

Eventually, Dane was the one to pull away. 'Like I said, this is a promise. I know we've only just met, but I know I want you to be a part of my life.'

Warm shivers fired in her stomach as his hand caressed her arms. His touch was pure magic, and she'd never felt anything like it before.

'I'm going to have to go to get back before dark,' he said reluctantly. 'But I bought something for you when we stopped in Normanton. So, I don't have to worry quite so much about you.'

'Show me,' she said softly.

His arms went around her waist again as his lips returned to hers. Nicole closed her eyes and a soft chuckle puffed out of her lips. 'I didn't know you could buy that at a shop.'

Dane stepped back, and his face was flushed, but his eyes were happy. 'Minx. I'll be back in a minute.'

Nicole stood with her fingers against her lips, willing her heart to slow down. Her thoughts were scattered, but it was so good to feel something other than fear. She watched as he went to the car and then bounded up the steps two at a time.

'It's only a cheap one, so don't go saying you won't accept it. You can give it back to me when you move out of here. It's in my name so there's no fear of it being linked to you. Okay?' He pulled his hand from behind his back and handed her a small mobile phone. 'It didn't cost much more than flowers and chocolates, but I'll get them next time.'

She reached her hand out for it. 'I won't say no. Thank you. Will it work up here?'

In his other hand, he held a black case. 'It will with this. This little device turns it into a satellite phone. We use them on the charter boats and they work like a dream.'

'And that was more expensive than flowers and chocolates, I'd say?'

'That one was more along the lines of dinner at an expensive restaurant, and we'll do that one day. I promise.'

'Thank you.'

Dane slapped his hand against his forehead, but his grin was wide. 'Is this Nicole who's standing in front of me? She's not arguing?'

Nicole shook her head and held out her hand for him to hold it. 'Do me one favour, Dane?'

'Yes?' His eyes were dark.

'Call me Nic. I liked it.'

Chapter 17

The week passed quickly and despite an early restlessness, Nicole and Binnie settled back into their routine. Binnie chatted more and more each day, and the only thing pressing on Nicole was the fear that one day she would ask about Laura. She had memories, and the mention of her "other" mummy, stayed with Nicole. The pottery was coming along well, and she'd been able to fire and glaze a dozen plates with the clay that she had already had on hand.

She lifted one to the light. The blues were beautiful, with a touch of deep green as she tipped it to the side. Hopefully, Helen would be pleased with them. As she picked up the brush and painted the glaze on the side of the last plate for the day, her thoughts turned to Dane and his family.

Well, not turned, she admitted to herself. Dane McDougal had been in her thoughts—both sleeping and waking—since he'd left five nights ago.

At first, she'd tried to resist thinking about him, and then had let her thoughts explore the unfamiliar feelings that he'd raised in her. In her twenty-five years, she'd had two boyfriends and had slept with only one of them in the first year she'd gone to art college.

But the feelings that ran rampant through her at Dane's touch, at his look, at his cheeky grin, and even thinking about him, were feelings she'd never experienced before.

She tried to analyse them, but couldn't, because every time she thought of them, Dane was in her head and the feeling came back.

She thought of his family and wondered why they were so keen to help her, be kind to her, and look out for her. It was not what she was used to. She and Laura had fended for themselves since their mother had passed away when Laura was in her last year of high school and Nicole had been at art college. Neither of them remembered their father; he'd left when Laura was two.

Their mother's family had left Mum well off and that inheritance had passed down to the two girls when she'd died; they'd never wanted for anything.

Nothing, except normal loving relationships, like she'd now seen in Dane's family. No wonder she and Laura had been ripe for Bruno's picking.

Laura would never have the opportunity of having a loving relationship, and she wouldn't see her beautiful little girl grow up A tear splashed onto her hand and Nicole wiped it away on her shorts. She stood staring out at the sea and vowed that she would provide a normal family life for Binnie. The fact that Dane's face sat squarely in her thoughts didn't surprise her.

Nor did it bother her.

But it was early days. She would wait and see what developed.

##

It was late in the afternoon and Binnie had woken up from her sleep, and it was almost time to cook their dinner. Nicole was feeling stronger; they had more food in the cupboards and camp fridge than they'd ever had, and they hadn't had to catch fish since they'd come back. She smiled as she had to move the block of chocolate in the fridge to reach the sausages she'd thawed for dinner.

An unfamiliar sound drifted in the window as she went to turn the gas on, and she paused.

'Bin, turn the light off, please.'

Binnie did as she was instructed immediately. They'd played this game before. Nicole walked over in the dark and took her hand. 'It might be time for a game of hide and seek,' she said quietly.

In the event of an emergency, she'd found a perfect hiding spot in the house, and she and Binnie had practised hiding in there. Nicole had made it a game to see how long they could be silent. No matter how unlikely it seemed that Bruno would find them, she always believed that he would find them one day.

She took Binnie to the side of the old gas range and watched as she crawled to the alcove behind it. 'Mummy's just going to look out the window and then I'll come in too. Now you be quiet and count like you've learned too, under your breath. Okay?'

The last view of Binnie was chubby little legs and a shorts-covered bottom crawling along the side of the stove.

Nicole crossed to the window and stood to the side. It was a motor that she could hear, and it was getting louder.

Like a motorbike. She shuddered. Bruno had ridden a huge powerful motorbike when he'd first taken Laura out.

The sickness began in her stomach, and she pushed her fist against her mouth as she peered through the window out to the road at the end of the driveway.

But there were no lights sweeping the night sky. As she turned back to the kitchen, flickering light to the north caught her attention. There was a large boat with red and green lights moving along the front of the bay. As she stared at the horizon, her eyes still adjusting to the dark, a smaller light moved into the shore. A flashlight danced on the water close to the edge of the bay.

Dane?

Nicole moved silently to the alcove. 'Stay there till I come back. Okay, Bin?'

'I will,' came the whisper, 'but now you've made me lose count.'

'Start again,' she whispered.

Nicole used the door at the back of the kitchen to go out and stand in the shadows on the veranda. Her heart was beating a low and steady beat, but her senses were on high alert.

She was fairly sure it was Dane, but until she was sure, she wouldn't show herself.

The sound of a metal hull scraping up the rocky beach broke the still night air.

The small yip that followed brought a smile to her lips.

It *was* Dane, and he'd brought Bits with him.

Her eyes adjusted to the dark, and she watched as he secured the small boat to a tree, holding Bits with his other hand. Her stomach curled with anticipation as he strode towards the house.

Before he reached the top of the stairs, she stepped out from the shadows.

'Hello, Dane.'

'Oh, thank God.' He put the pup down and it was only two steps until he reached her and took her in his arms. His hands were shaking as he held her close and he buried his face in her hair.

'It's okay. I heard the motor, so I hid Binnie. It's okay, Dane. We're here and safe.' It was so different to be reassuring him for a change.

His voice was rough. 'I thought you'd left. When the house was in darkness, I was sure of it.' His lips pressed against hers in a desperate kiss. 'I thought you'd left. I thought I'd come on too strong and fast.'

'We're here. If we were going to leave, I'd tell you.'

'Promise?' His lips were firm and cool against hers as he elicited the promise.

'I promise. Why were you so worried?'

'Because I've been trying to call you on that phone for the past two nights and it rang out.'

Nicole looked up surprised. 'It hasn't rung.'

'Has it gone flat?' Finally, a hint of a smile in his tone.

'I don't know. I left it on the bench and I haven't looked at it again. I did plug it all in like you showed me.'

Dane took her hand and they walked inside. Nicole flicked the kitchen light on and bent down. 'We have two visitors, Bin.'

There was a squeal and a chuckle at the same time. Binnie's squeal as Bits sniffed out her hiding spot and Dane's quiet chuckle behind her. 'It's flat.'

Nicole swung around. 'But it's plugged in?'

'It is, but the switch has been turned off.'

'Oh,' she said sheepishly. 'Sorry, it's ages since I had a phone, and besides no one was going to ring us.'

'I tried.'

'Oh.' Nicole crossed to the stove. 'Come on out, you pair. We have to get some dinner on for our visitors.'

'I hope that's an invitation,' Dane said.

'Do you have much time?'

The slow lazy curl of his lips sent a quiver darting straight downwards. 'I'm on watch at

183

midnight.' He looked down at his wristwatch. 'And that is a whole six hours away.'

***

Nicole had cooked a pasta dish with sausage and garlic, and to cater for the third person at the table had thrown a salad together. Binnie and Bits were fast asleep on the mattress in the bedroom; he'd helped her drag the other one out of the bedroom and into the living room. He leaned against the wall with his legs stretched out in front of him. After comparing each other's weeks, the conversation turned to more general topics.

'I can't believe you've never been out to sea,' he said shaking his head. Nicole was leaning back against his chest and each time she spoke her head moved and her fine hair tickled his chin. His arms were looped around her, and he was trying to keep the conversation going because all he wanted to do was kiss her senseless.

If he was honest, that's not all he wanted. But with a young child in the house, it wouldn't be right.

And it was too soon.

Dane was in the middle of asking her a question when Nicole moved suddenly. One minute he was chatting away and the next . . .

He swallowed as she turned quickly and straddled his thighs; he stared into the heavy eyes of a woman oozing sex appeal.

'Um, what are you doing?' he managed to choke out as her hands slipped beneath his T-shirt.

'Something I've been wanting to do for the past two hours.' Even her voice was different—low and throaty.

God help him. Her knees were either side of his thighs and she was moving even closer. He swallowed as the blood surged through his body. 'Binnie?'

'Is sound asleep.'

'You're not playing fair.' He could barely get the words out as the blood left his brain and travelled elsewhere.

'Fair or not doesn't matter. This is what I want. What we want?'

With a groan, he moved quickly and rolled over so that Nicole was lying beneath him. The smile on her lips was wide as he lowered his mouth to hers.

Chapter 18

Nicole hummed under her breath as she worked on the first platter early the next afternoon. Despite the late night, she'd woken early. Dane had left with about ten minutes to spare before he was due on watch. Neither Binnie nor Bits had stirred as Dane and Nicole showered together just before midnight, their laughter and talking kept as low as possible.

She had walked him to the small boat, despite his protests about crocodiles, but had given in and stood well away from the shore as he'd pushed the boat into the water.

But not until he'd kissed her thoroughly first.

'I'll be up in three days,' he promised. 'Hopefully, your clay has arrived, and I can bring it with me.'

'Wait until it comes before you make the trip,' she said.

'No. I'll want to see *you*. Don't argue.'

'Yes, sir,' she'd said with a smile that didn't want to go away.

As expected, Binnie squealed with delight for a good half hour when she discovered Bits had come for a visit. Now she was curled up with him and having her afternoon sleep; Dane had left Bits behind saying it would keep the little girl entertained while Nicole worked.

She picked up a piece of sandpaper and worked away at the rough spots that had remained on the platter after the firing. With a grunt of satisfaction, she held it up; the shape was perfect. Now to get the glaze on; it might be best to leave it until she'd woken Binnie and Bits and they'd had their afternoon tea.

As Nicole mixed up some cereal for the pup and Binnie, the combined yips and squeals were so loud, she almost missed the phone ringing.

'Ssh.' She picked up the phone with a smile, expecting it to be Dane, but it was a woman's voice.

'Hello, this is Jill from the Tourist Information Centre. Could I speak to Dane please?'

Nicole hesitated. 'I'm sorry. He's not here at the moment.'

'Is that you, Jenni? I'm after your Mum.'

Nicole muffled her voice and put her hand half over the phone. 'Sorry not here either.' She should never have answered the phone. Whoever he'd bought it off must have recorded Dane's name as the owner and passed it on.

Small towns!

'Okay, love. Can you tell her to call me, please? There's been a fellow here a few times, looking for that potter lady. Nicole, I think her name is. He's been persistent, and he's just left. I said that your Mum will know where to find her.'

Nicole's blood ran cold, and she dropped the phone without replying.

Two people knew where to find her. Dane and *his mother.*

She closed her eyes and put her hand to her mouth.

Was it Bruno? How had he tracked her? The only way she could think was through her PayPal account and that had led him straight to the Normanton post office. Would he have come himself, or would he have sent one of his thugs?

Panic built in her chest as her thoughts skittered around. Her pulse was racing, and a sharp pain was building at the base of her throat.

They had to leave.

Now.

Before Helen told him where to find her. As far as she knew, Helen knew nothing about Bruno or Laura. Dane was at sea and couldn't help her, but all she wanted was to talk to him and tell him why she had to leave. She couldn't contact him without going through his family, and she didn't want to raise an alarm with anyone else.

If Bruno came here, they'd be sitting ducks and she well knew what he was capable of. Dane knew how dangerous he was and—

Nicole bit back a groan as Bits ran into the kitchen closely followed by Binnie.

Damn, she was going to have to take the dog with her. The chickens were all gone, and she didn't have to worry about them. A snake had got to them while she was at Dane's place last week.

She took a deep breath and began to plan their escape.

***

One of the passengers had taken ill, and Dane had decided to cut the trip short. It was a family group who'd booked the charter, so they were all happy to go back to Second Chance Bay while they sought medical attention for the oldest member of the family who had suffered stomach pains. He wasn't sick enough to be medi-vacced off the boat but was too sick for the trip to continue. Dane had radioed ahead to Matt and let him know they were coming in, and Matt and Jake were waiting at the dock with the paramedics when he brought the *Elsie* down the river in the afternoon.

It took less than half an hour to disembark the passengers. He walked into the office with Matt and Jake while the deckies scrubbed down the boat and offloaded the rubbish.

'A couple of days off again, hey mate?' Jake said. 'You've had it easy over the past couple of weeks. How's the new place going? Jenni said you've been up there a couple of times.'

'Yeah. It should be good. I'm still thinking about what to do.'

'Want some company next time you go up? I wouldn't mind having a look.'

'Yeah, sure.' It was easier to agree now and come up with an excuse later.

Matt went across to the small fridge and opened the door. 'Beers?'

Dane held his hand out for a beer, but Matt paused. 'Oh, I forgot. There was a message for you from Mum when you were coming through the heads.'

'What about?'

Matt shrugged. 'I don't know. She said to tell you it was urgent, and it was something to do with a Nicole or some name like that.'

Both Matt and Jake's mouths dropped open as Dane pushed past them and ran for the door.

##

'I didn't know what to say, love.' Helen was in the kitchen at the pub basting a roast that had been cooking for a while by the delicious aroma that pervaded the dining room. 'I knew I couldn't say too much, so I said I'd get back to him. He's a very nice man.'

Dane snorted. 'Not from what I've heard. What did he say his name was?'

Helen turned to the bench and dug into her handbag. She read the card before she passed it to Dane. 'Gareth Scholes. He's from Melbourne. He said it's imperative that he speak to a Nicole Smyth. When he described her I knew it was your Nicole.'

'Smyth?' Dane looked down and read the card. 'Where's he staying?

'In the motel next to the airport. Maybe she's come into some money or something.'

'Maybe.' Dane didn't want to frighten his mother. 'I'll go and see him.'

***

It only took an hour to pack what Nicole needed to take with them. Lifting the camp fridge while loaded had been impossible, and it added an extra ten minutes while she unpacked it, carried it to the car and then reloaded it. Binnie's eyes were wide, and her bottom lip quivered.

Bloody heck. She was so intuitive.

'We're just going on a little trip, sweetie, so get your pencils and your Bits Two.'

'What about this Bits? Can he come too?'

191

Nicole nodded. 'Now hurry up and go and get your things. I've packed your new clothes and we'll get going.'

As she drove south she worried about what to do. She only had a thousand dollars in cash, not enough to head off and set up somewhere else. Maybe she could just lie low for a while. As far as she could make out, whoever was looking for her was in Normanton. If she took the turn off before town, she could bypass Normanton and head for the Bay, drop Bits off and maybe—if the offer was still going—take up the offer of that house that Dane had wanted to show her. She and Binnie could get the boat over and stay inside and no one needed to know they were there. It wasn't an ideal solution, but it was the best she could come up with, with limited money.

The problem she had to overcome was that Dane wasn't onshore for another two days. She bit her lip as she took the turn north of Normanton and headed for Second Chance Bay. There was a motel up the road from the pub near the airport. She would see if they had a vacant room and then drop Bits off with Helen.

And hide.

***

Dane sat in the conference room at the front of the hotel and shook his head in disbelief as he stared at the man opposite him. His mother had been right; Gareth Scholes was a good man and his motivation came from a place that Dane had never imagined.

'At the pub up the road, you say. Now?'

Gareth nodded. 'Yes. So, are you prepared to tell me where Nicole is?'

Dane ran a hand through his hair. 'I need to talk to her first. I tried to call her, but she's not answering her phone. 'I'll have to go and get her, but we won't be back until tomorrow.'

'So, you're not prepared to tell me where she is?'

He shook his head. 'It's not up to me to make that decision. Mate, you've blown me away by what you've told me. Tell me, how did you track her to here?'

'An eBay order. A PayPal payment and a delivery to the post office at Normanton. And then we tracked the pottery order to the pub here via the Tourism Office.'

'So much for privacy these days. Nicole had reason to be scared.'

Gareth frowned. 'I'll be honest with you, Dane. I'm not an investigator or anything. Just someone with IT skills who knows how to hack into systems. For the right reasons.'

Dane heard a car door slam and he automatically glanced at the window. The hair on the back of his neck stood to attention and he widened his eyes as he stared. He half stood, and the chair fell to the floor behind him with a crash. Gareth turned and followed his gaze.

Dane ran for the door, closely followed by the other man.

Nicole had just opened the front door and climbed in, and now her dark green Subaru was heading up the road towards the hotel.

'Bloody hell, we need to catch her,' he yelled. 'Where's your car? I walked down from the pub.'

Gareth ran beside him to the car park adjacent to the small airport.

***

There had been a room at the pub for two nights and then Nicole decided she'd reconsider her options when Dane came home. First job was to drop Bits off, and then park the car around the back of the motel and hide out. She felt conspicuous in her car. Although the sun had set, it was still light enough to see. Too many people knew it was hers. They had enough food to bunker down in the motel for a week if need be. She parked at the side of the hotel and grabbed her bag. There was too much money in there to let it out of her sight.

Before Nicole could get out of the car, Binnie had wriggled out of her seat, picked up Bits and pushed open the door. She was weaving her way through the tables towards the one on the lawn where they'd sat last time.

'Binnie, wait.' She put her head down and took off after the little girl and the pup.

In one instant her world went crazy.

She'd almost caught up to Binnie and Bits when Dane yelled out her name. 'Nicole?'

At the same time, Helen walked out of the kitchen, and her eyes were wide as she gestured to Dane.

Fear twisted Nicole's insides as a woman screamed from the table beside her; she turned slowly as the woman lunged for Binnie.

'Binnie, Binnie,' the woman sobbed as her arms went around the little girl and Bits took off.

Their little girl.

Her little girl.

Dane caught her as her knees buckled and she looked into the face of her sister.

'Laura?'

Epilogue

12 months later

Nicole held the plate up to the light and frowned; there was a hair from the paintbrush set in the glaze. With a soft sigh, she put the piece on the table on the side of the verandah. It had to be perfect for every order she did. Near enough wasn't good enough.

It was a glorious day on the Gulf. A huge flock of magpie geese had flown over at dawn, heading for the wetlands down near the river, and woken her in time to see the Morning Glory roll cloud. It had been spectacular this morning and had filled her with inspiration for a new series of bowls. Now the only sound was the rhythmic banging of hammers at the far end of the beach as the builders finished off the last of the lodges.

It had taken Nicole a few months of Binnie not being there to get used to the quiet. Sometimes, she still caught herself wondering what she'd cook her little niece for dinner, but those days were getting few and far between as the weeks passed.

She had plenty to keep her occupied. New commissions, new lodges and a man she loved more as each day passed.

Jake's *Moonshine*, with Dane onboard, was due to dock at the new jetty in an hour. Even without the lodges being open—the grand opening was next weekend—the charters had been full, with a waiting list for bookings stretching months ahead. The familiar frisson of excitement as Dane's homecoming grew closer started in her toes and worked its way up to her heart. This afternoon, the workers were catching the boat back to Weipa and a weekend of solitude, with just the two of them here to wander around their new resort, beckoned.

'We'll make the most of it this weekend, sweetheart, because the lodges are fully booked for six months after the opening next weekend,' Dane had promised as he'd left on the boat with Jake five days ago. 'And I've got something to run by you and we need time to talk it over.'

Nicole had been curious, but he hadn't said any more.

Everyone was coming up for the grand opening, and it still surprised her how quickly she'd become used to being a part of Dane's family after almost eighteen months of living in the wilderness alone with Binnie.

Gareth, Laura, and Binnie were flying up next Friday for the grand opening and she was looking forward to seeing them. Laura had met Gareth at a bereaved parents' group—she had believed that Bruno had found Nicole and Binnie after he'd shot her. It had been Gareth who had encouraged her to search for them, and he had helped her for the six months until he'd tracked Nicole's PayPal transaction.

The day that Laura arrived in Second Chance Bay was imprinted on Nicole's memory forever. The sheer happiness of seeing her sister alive and well, with only a small scar where the bullet had scarred her forehead to remind her of that dreadful day, had overcome all Nicole's fear, and the difficulty of being with people. Hearing that Bruno had also died that day—a shotgun death after a gangland drug deal gone wrong—had filled her with sorrow. Not for his death, but the fact that she'd left Laura, thinking she was dead when she'd needed her most, and then taken Binnie from her mother for over a year.

And she hadn't needed to.

By the time Laura had regained consciousness in the hospital, Nicole and Binnie had been long gone.

Gareth had shaken his head when they had all settled down that day. 'You did a damn good job of hiding and keeping her safe, Nicole. It's taken me six months to find you.'

'I'm so sorry, Laura,' she'd said. 'I couldn't feel your pulse and I thought the worst. I called triple zero and got Binnie out of there before he came back.' Her control had slipped, and she'd sobbed. 'I didn't know what to do. I should have stayed with you.'

'But Bruno might have come back, and then where would we have been?' Laura had wrapped her in her arms. 'You did the right thing, honey. You called emergency. And having Gareth help me this year has had a happy ending.' She looked at the man standing beside her with a wide smile. 'We're getting married next year, and now we have Binnie, we can be a family.'

Rather than hiding away in a motel, the night at the hotel had turned into a celebration as the rest of Dane's family had joined them.

Nicole headed for the shower in the newly refurbished bathroom in the beautiful old house. When she'd agreed to move in with Dane after she'd come back from Melbourne—she'd only lasted there for three weeks—he'd organised to have the house renovated, and they'd moved to the house at the Bay for three months.

The graceful old Queenslander that Nicole told Laura was her outback haven, was now painted in a soft white and had a new roof. As well as a new kitchen being installed, the interior floors had been polished, and Dane had replaced the verandah floor, railings and stairs so that they looked the same as the original design.

But the best part was the new studio at the end of the verandah, next to the office that Dane had added as the reception area for the new lodges.

As she dried her hair, the loud blast of *Moonshine*'s horn rang across the water. Quickly pulling on a short floral dress, Nicole closed the door behind her and ran down the stairs.

The workmen had packed up their gear and were waiting to board as the boat came to the wharf. Dane was standing up at the wheelhouse and she smiled when he blew her a kiss. She waved back and waited for the boat to dock.

Dane and Jake walked down the gangway together and after greeting the workers, Dane hurried across, lifted Nicole from her feet and kissed her. 'I've missed you, Nic.'

'It's been a long week here, too,' she said linking her arms around his neck.

They stood close together as the workers boarded the boat.

'We'll see you in a few days for the big weekend,' Jake said as he walked back up the gangway. 'Apparently, Helen's got the catering under control, according to Jenni.' He gave them a wave as the deckie undid the ropes. 'See you soon.'

Dane and Nicole walked to their house hand-in-hand. Streaks of gold, overlaid with indigo lit the sky, and the sea faded to silver near the shore, deepening to burnt orange as the sun sank slowly to the horizon.

As they reached the bottom of the staircase, he turned to Nicole. 'I can't wait any longer. I've been practising this for five days and I'm so nervous I need to get it out. Now.'

Nicole frowned. 'What's wrong? Practising what?'

Dane put one hand gently on each side of her waist and stared down at her. 'I met a beautiful woman on this very spot a year ago. She was Nicole Curtis and then I found out she was really Nicole Smyth, after she'd been hijacked for a short and forgettable time as Nicoletta Spagnolo.'

Nicole smiled. 'Confusing, wasn't I?'

Dane reached into the pocket of his shorts and pulled out a black case. 'I've thought of a way to get rid of all of that confusion, Nic.' He flicked open the case and Nicole stared at the beautiful ring that was nestled in dark blue satin. A pink diamond winked up at her.

'I found the ring I wanted in a catalogue, and Donny collected it for me from the Kimberley diamond store last week and gave it to Jake who brought it up to me from Second Chance Bay.'

'A ring?' She swallowed.

'I'd like you to be Nicole McDougal. What do you think?'

She smiled as Dane took the ring and slipped it onto her finger

'I love you, Nic.'

Nicole reached up and held his loving gaze as she gently pulled his head down towards hers. No more words were necessary as the sun slipped below the horizon in a glorious flash of gold.

THE END

If you enjoy reading about the McDougal family, Her Outback Paradise (Matt's story) is available now

Matt McDougal looks after the family fishing business. He takes the bookings, runs the store and looks after the finances … because he gets seasick on the charter boats. When nurse, Sara Sweeney, comes back to her home town she entices her doctor friend, Caroline, to come with her to remote Second Chance Bay to work with the one doctor in town. Matt and Sara grew up together, and a broken relationship in the city has destroyed Sara's trust. When Sara and Caroline arrive in town, Sara thinks Matt would be a perfect partner for her friend, and it will also entice Caroline to stay in the remote area. But Matt has already lost Sara once, can he convince her now, he is the right man for her?

Acknowledgments

A special thank you to my wonderful editor and critique partner, Susanne Bellamy.

You polish my sentences until they shine.

Have you read:
Beach House

From award-winning author Annie Seaton, this romance will make you smile.

Rosie Pemberton has her life mapped out, and her tarot cards agree. The cards take a turn, though, when her aunt leaves the old house on the hill above Australia's Bondi Beach to champion surfer Taj Brown. Three months of sharing a house with a pinup would test any woman's self-control…

Also by Annie Seaton

Whitsunday Dawn
Undara
Osprey Reef
East of Alice (November 2022)

Porter Sisters Series
Kakadu Sunset
Daintree
Diamond Sky
Hidden Valley
Larapinta

Pentecost Island Series
Pippa
Eliza
Nell
Tamsin
Evie
Cherry
Odessa
Sienna
Tess
Also available in three boxed sets
Books 1-3
Books 4-6
Books 7-10

The Augathella Girls Series
Outback Roads
Outback Sky
Outback Escape
Outback Wind
Outback Dawn
Outback Moonlight
Outback Dust
Outback Hope

Sunshine Coast Series
Waiting for Ana
The Trouble with Jack
Healing His Heart
Sunshine Coast Boxed Set

The Richards Brothers Series
The Trouble with Paradise
Marry in Haste
Outback Sunrise
Richards Brothers Boxed Set

Bondi Beach Love Series
Beach House
Beach Music
Beach Walk
Beach Dreams
The House on the Hill

Second Chance Bay Series
Her Outback Playboy

Her Outback Protector
Her Outback Haven
Her Outback Paradise
The McDougalls of Second Chance Bay Boxed Set

Love Across Time Series
Come Back to Me
Follow Me
Finding Home
The Threads that Bind
Love Across Time 1-4 Boxed Set

Bindarra Creek
Worth the Wait
Full Circle
Secrets of River Cottage (Nov 22)

Four Seasons Short and Sweet
Ten Days in Paradise
Follow the Sun

Others
Deadly Secrets
Adventures in Time
Silver Valley Witch
The Emerald Necklace
Christmas with the Boss
Her Christmas Star
An Aussie Christmas Duo (the two Christmas novellas)

About the Author

Author of the Year Ausrom Readers' Choice 2014

Best Established Author Ausrom Readers' Choice 2015

Finalist for Author of the Year, Book of the Year, Cover of the Year, Ausrom Readers' Choice 2016

Best Established Author, Ausrom Readers' Choice 2017

Book of the Year (Whitsunday Dawn) Ausrom Readers' Choice 2018

Annie lives in Australia, on the beautiful north coast of New South Wales. She sits in her writing chair and looks out over the tranquil Pacific Ocean. She has fulfilled her lifelong dream of becoming an author and is producing books at a prolific rate.

She writes contemporary romance and loves telling stories that always have a happily ever after. She lives with her very own hero of many years and they share their home with Toby, the naughtiest dog in the universe, and Barney, the rag doll kitten, who hides when the grandchildren come to visit.

Stay up to date with her latest releases at her website: http://www.annieseaton.net

If you would like to stay up to date with Annie's releases, subscribe to her newsletter here: http://www.annieseaton.net

www.ingramcontent.com/pod-product-compliance
Lightning Source LLC
Chambersburg PA
CBHW030646110726
47901CB00002B/587